JOY TO THE DUKE

USA TODAY
BESTSELLING AUTHOR

DARCY BURKE

JOY TO THE DUKE

Denied the woman of his dreams by his father's meddling, Calder Stafford, has spent the last decade proving himself to be self-sufficient, austere, and utterly uninterested in joy. Now that he is the Duke of Hartwell, he'll enact his revenge by abolishing the holiday traditions his father loved so well. His sisters will not sway him and neither will the woman—newly returned to town—who was stolen from him.

Returning to Hartwell to care for her mother, widow Felicity Garland is delighted to be back home, especially for the holidays. However, the jolly festivities she expects are nowhere to be found. When she goes to the source of the problem —the duke—she's astonished to see how much the young man she once loved has hardened. It's up to her to break through the impenetrable fortress around his heart—not just to save Christmas, but to save *him*.

Don't miss the rest of Love is All Around, a Regency Holiday Trilogy!

Book one: The Red Hot Earl
Book two: The Gift of the Marquess
Book three: Joy to the Duke

Love romance? Have a free book (or two or three) on me!

Sign up at http://www.darcyburke.com/readerclub for members-only exclusives, including advance notice of pre-orders and insider scoop, as well as contests, giveaways, freebies, and 99 cent deals!

Want to share your love of my books with like-minded readers? Want to hang with me and get inside scoop? Then don't miss my exclusive Facebook groups!

Darcy's Duchesses for historical readers
Burke's Book Lovers for contemporary readers

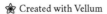 Created with Vellum

For my children, who are the very definition of joy

CHAPTER 1

County Durham, England
December 1811

$\mathcal{F}$elicity was back.

Calder strode from the drawing room at his estate, Hartwood, via the same doorway his younger sisters had just used to depart. But he didn't follow them. He went in search of a footman and sent him to the stables to see that a groom saddled his horse. After sending another footman to fetch his greatcoat, hat, and gloves, Calder made his way outside. A short while later, he raced toward the village of Hartwell.

Founded in the Middle Ages, Hartwell was built around a center market square. The spire of St. Cuthbert's, the twelfth-century church, stood sentinel over the quaint gathering of shops and cottages.

With the holiday season upon them, doors and windows were decorated with festive greenery. There was, all around, an aura of good cheer. It did not, however, permeate Calder's carefully constructed exterior. Words such as "quaint" and "festive" and "joy" had no place in his heart.

The mere thought of that organ made his squeeze. Or, more likely, it was the knowledge that Felicity Templeton—no, she was Felicity Garland now—was near.

Calder knew her mother had returned to Hartwell last year, but he'd gone out of his way to avoid her. Even so, he was aware of precisely where she lived. How else could he be certain to steer clear of her?

Turning his horse down Kingston Street, he eyed Mrs. Templeton's cottage farther down the road. Like its neighbors, the home was festooned with pine boughs. Smoke wafted from the chimney, rising above the thatched roof.

Now what?

He realized he didn't know what he meant to do. Speak to her? He shuddered inwardly at the thought. Felicity had run off over a decade ago, breaking his heart.

Yet, he had plenty he wanted to say to her. His mind raged with questions and anger. Why had she left without a word?

Except he knew why. His father had paid her family, securing their future so that marriage to the heir to a dukedom wasn't necessary. It appeared that had been her only motivation in attaching herself to him in courtship. Not love or attraction or affection of any kind—she'd been driven purely by avarice.

Calder took a deep breath. Cold winter air filled his lungs, freezing his insides the way everyone presumed they were. He had a heart of ice and a hollow soul. So they said.

And they weren't wrong.

A figure stepped out of the cottage, followed by

another. Calder moved his horse to a side lane, positioning himself behind a tree.

The two women passed through the gate into the street and linked arms. Even from this distance, Felicity was precisely as he remembered. Tall and graced with curves that could make a man weep with want, her features were so finely honed, surely every artist in the kingdom should want to paint her. Blonde curls peeked from beneath the rim of her bonnet. She laughed at something her mother said, the lilting song of her voice somehow easing the ache inside him.

Only for a moment. As she moved along the street on the other side, he saw her face more clearly—the delicate arch of her brows, the gentle sweep of her nose, the sculpted beauty of her cheekbones and jawline. But his gaze settled on her mouth, with its lush pink lips that could kiss and seduce him like no one else.

Not that she'd *actually* seduced him, not completely. He'd anticipated taking her to bed when they wed. That dream had died. Or, perhaps more accurately, had been stolen.

Still, he feasted on her, his gaze moving hungrily over her to memorize every new detail—the crinkles around her eyes when she smiled, the air of confidence and perhaps wisdom, the smart way she surveyed her surroundings.

Bloody hell. She was looking this way.

Calder turned his horse and cantered down the lane toward Shield Street, the main thoroughfare that cut through the village. His heart beat quickly, and, if he were honest, he would realize it wasn't due to the ride. But he refused to allow it to be because of Felicity. He'd seen her, and that was enough.

Except, knowing she was near was likely to be a fracture in his mind.

"Good afternoon, Your Grace."

Calder had slowed his mount as he'd turned onto Shield Street. Blinking, he pulled himself from the dark pit of his thoughts and focused on the man addressing him. Alfie Tucket, the cabinet-maker, stood outside his shop. He bowed, bending his tall form before straightening once more.

"Good afternoon," Calder said. He might be a blackguard, but he was also polite. Sometimes.

"On your way to Shield's End?" Tucket asked, blinking as he looked up at Calder on his horse.

Calder realized he'd been riding in that direction—the old house stood at the end of Shield Street, hence its name. Rather, it *had* stood. The structure had burned over a week ago.

"No," he answered, even as he considered going to see it. Beyond his curiosity, he should care about the destruction since the property belonged to his brother-in-law. The man he'd forbidden his sister to marry.

And whom she'd wed last week.

Tucket shifted his weight, looking slightly un-comfortable. His father was the caretaker at Shield's End. It was possible, if not likely, that Tucket knew that Calder hadn't visited the dam-aged house and that he hadn't attended his sister's wedding.

There it was again. That sharp, brief twinge in his chest. Though he didn't react, Calder never failed to register the sensation.

Calder turned his horse once more and rode in the opposite direction from Shield's End, toward Hartwood, which stood atop a hill that overlooked the village. The dukes of Hartwell had lived there for centuries. Would they still?

Only if Calder married, and though he was now thirty, he couldn't be moved to take a wife. Not when Felicity still lived in the recesses of his mind.

Time to evict her, his mind chided.

He thought he had, but now that she was here… He shook his head. Perhaps he could find a way to make her leave again. Or, if he were lucky, her stay would only be temporary.

Arriving at the Hartwood stable, Calder turned the care of his horse, something he typically saw to himself, over to a groom. A ripple of unease ran through him. He needed to walk. Curling his tongue, he whistled. A moment later, his dark red-brown greyhound bounded to his side.

Calder stroked the dog's head, scratching her behind the ears. As Calder set off from the stable yard, Isis fell in beside him. They walked past the gardens to where the hill began to slope. Nestled at the base was the family crypt, a place Calder never went.

There lay tragedy and pain—a parent he missed with every fiber of his being and another he loathed with equal vehemence.

The question that had come to his mind earlier returned: would there be any more dukes of Hartwell? He ought to ensure there weren't, at least not from his line. There had to be a cousin somewhere who would inherit. It would serve Calder's father right to have the title pass to some distant relative. Or to pass to no one at all.

The chill in Calder's heart hardened to stone as he thought of the man who'd raised him. The man everyone else remembered fondly, particularly his sisters. They hadn't been subjected to his high expectations, his ruthless demands for perfection at all costs. He hadn't paid the men they'd fallen in love with to leave and then crowed about how right he'd been about them all along.

The twinge pinched his chest again. Perhaps he should have supported his sister's marriage. He barely knew her husband, the Earl of Buckleigh, but from what he'd seen, the man was a volatile fighter, a pugilist regarded for his efficient brutality in the ring. And yet, he couldn't see his sweet, fierce youngest sister, Bianca, marrying someone like that.

Calder ran his gloved fingers over Isis's head. "It doesn't matter, does it, girl?" he asked softly. "He wanted me to be a beast, and so I am."

Isis nudged his hand in response then sat down beside him, content just to be next to him. She might be the actual beast, but she was far kinder and more loving than he.

"I don't really deserve you," he murmured.

He looked down into her large brown eyes that gazed at him so adoringly. Squatting, he stroked her neck and sides with both hands. Then he looked back toward the crypt and spoke to the man he despised.

"I am alone, and I shall probably remain that way. I hope that taunts you for an eternity."

Calder rose and turned, striding back toward the house with Isis trotting alongside him.

Yes, his father had raised him to be ruthless and unyielding. And since Calder strove to excel in everything, that meant he was as cold and unforgiving as one could be.

~

 ou look lovely, dear."

Felicity donned her cloak just before opening the door for her mother.

"Thank you, as do you, Mama." She picked up the small bag, which held her dancing slippers—Mama wouldn't be dancing since she was still somewhat recovering from her illness—and followed her mother out into the cold, dark evening.

"I'm so looking forward to the assembly," Mama said as Felicity linked arms with her. "How many years has it been?"

"Ten." Felicity recalled the last assembly she'd attended in Hartwell. She'd been eighteen and so eager to see her love when he came home from Oxford for the holiday. They'd spent the prior summer together, enjoying every moment possible in each other's company, dreaming of the future in the warmth from the sun and from the passion of their stolen kisses.

Only, he hadn't come. His father had explained that he wouldn't be returning for the holidays, and he'd given her a letter. Brief and cold, the words written by her love had stated in plain terms that they had no future together.

When her father had suggested they move to York where her older brother would be practicing law, she'd leapt at the chance to leave Hartwell—and her broken heart—behind. She hadn't been back since.

"You came last year, didn't you?" Felicity glanced over at her mother, whose white-blonde hair was swept into a fashionable style, though it was partially obscured by the hood of her cloak, which she'd pulled up as they'd left the house. It was important she keep warm after having been ill. Her ailment had been the only thing that could draw Felicity back, and so here she was. She had to admit she'd missed the village and its people, especially at this time of year. Christmas in York couldn't come close to the charm and tradition of Hartwell.

"I did, but it wasn't the same without your father." She summoned a smile as she looked at Felicity. "And you." Mama reached over and patted Felicity's hand.

Papa had died last fall—it was hard to believe it had been over a year already. Awash in grief, Mama had wanted to escape from the house she'd shared with her husband for the past decade, where he'd fallen ill and died. Coming back to Hartwell, where she still had friends and a cousin, had made sense despite Felicity trying to dissuade her.

But that had been selfishness on Felicity's part. Hartwell, for all the good memories it held, would always be the place where she'd lost her innocence, where she'd been a fool to give her heart so completely.

"I'm so glad you're with me this year," Mama said, smiling. "And I do hope you're here to stay."

That was an ongoing debate. Felicity had a home and friends back in York. Yet, it was hard to deny her mother's request. Felicity had begun to hope she could talk *her* into returning to York and living with Felicity.

"Or you're going to come back to York with me. I know you miss your friends." Felicity flashed her a smile, and her mother laughed.

"Don't try to sway me with your father's charm. I am immune."

She wasn't either, but Felicity only chuckled in response.

Mama slid her a probing look. "Are you looking forward to seeing anyone in particular? You've kept to yourself for the most part since returning."

It had only been a handful of weeks, really. "I've been busy helping you."

"Yes, and I'm delighted to have you here with me. I know you are the reason for my recovery."

"Not entirely." Felicity knew her presence had helped. "Dr. Fisk had a great deal to do with it."

"You're right, of course. In fact, I wonder if he might have been able to help your father." Her voice turned sad. "We should have returned to Hartwell when he became sick."

Felicity squeezed her mother's arm gently. "You mustn't think like that. You told Dr. Fisk about Papa's illness, and he said there was likely nothing he could do, that you'd done your best to care for him."

"It's hard not to feel regret," Mama said softly. "But then you seem to be unaffected by that emotion."

Hardly. Felicity regretted more than she admitted, all of it to do with Calder Stafford. She'd almost thought of him as "Chill," the nickname from his youth when he'd been the Earl of Chilton. Now, however, he was the Duke of Hartwood. She'd never liked calling him Chill—the cool moniker hadn't made sense to her, not when she thought of him as so warm and caring.

How wrong she'd been.

They reached the assembly hall, where a line of carriages dropped off elegantly clad attendees. Light and conversation poured from the building, lending a festive air. A tremor of anxiousness rippled across Felicity's shoulders. She wasn't sure she was ready to face Calder.

She chided herself internally. She refused to be intimidated by him or the prospect of seeing him again. She was ten years older, widowed, and she'd lived on her own the past two years. The young girl he'd so callously hurt was long gone.

Holding her head high, she escorted her mother into the hall. In the vestibule, a footman took their outer garments, and Felicity swapped her boots for her dancing slippers.

They strolled into the ballroom, which was already quite full. Young ladies giggled in the corner, while a group of young bucks tried to appear composed as they surveyed the room, their gazes continually returning to the young ladies.

Felicity smiled to herself. She remembered what it felt like to be youthful and excited, anticipation for the future—the unknown—coursing through her.

They walked to an area on the other side of the ballroom that had been arranged with seating that provided an excellent view of the dance floor.

Eyeing a chair, Felicity inclined her head. "Come, Mama. You must sit. Otherwise, I will rethink my decision to allow you to come. You are still recovering."

"Oh, pooh. I'm fine, dear. But yes, a chair would not come amiss."

Turning her head slightly, Felicity saw a pair of familiar faces—Calder's sisters. Her heart paused as she glanced around in search of him. Not seeing him, she exhaled with relief as his sisters, along with a gentleman, came toward her. Felicity dipped into a curtsey. "Good evening Lady Darlington and Lady…Buckleigh, is it?"

"Yes," Bianca, Calder's youngest sister who had very recently wed the Earl of Buckleigh, answered. "Allow me to present my husband, the Earl of Buckleigh. Ash, this is Mrs. Felicity Garland." Her blue eyes glowed with warmth.

Ash inclined his head. "Of course I remember you, Mrs. Garland."

Surprise leapt through Felicity as she rose from her curtsey. "Ash, as in little Ashton Rutledge? I would not have recognized you."

"None of us did," Bianca said with a laugh, a dark curl grazing her temple.

"How marvelous to see you all." Felicity allowed her gaze to briefly scan the ballroom once more. "Where is your brother? I've yet to encounter him since I returned to Hartwell." She wasn't asking because she wanted to see him, but because if he were here, she wanted to know. To be on guard.

Poppy, the older of the two and the Marchioness of Darlington, and Bianca exchanged a wary look. "I doubt he'll be here this evening," Poppy answered. "He's not very social these days. The dukedom keeps him quite busy."

Felicity was shocked to feel a spark of disappointment. "That's too bad. I'd looked forward to seeing him. I suppose I'll just have to pay a call." The words came out because Felicity always endeavored to be polite. She had no intention of calling on him.

It appeared his sisters didn't think visiting was a good idea. Bianca snapped a look toward Poppy and opened her mouth to speak. However, Poppy cut her off, saying to Felicity, "Perhaps send him a note asking when he receives visitors." Her lips curved into a serene smile, likely meant to smooth any upset Felicity might have detected. Clearly, she wasn't imagining their discomfort.

The sound of the Earl of Buckleigh inhaling sharply drew Felicity's attention. But the earl was fixated on the entrance. "He's here." His tone was flat and yet the two simple words sliced through

Felicity with the quick, terrifying efficiency of a long sword from days of old.

Felicity felt her mother pat her arm, but her gaze was trained on Calder. Tall, with broad shoulders that had once made her swoon, he filled the doorway. His crystalline eyes swept over the assembly, his expression impassive.

Had the ballroom gone quiet? Not entirely, for there was a faint buzzing in Felicity's ears as she beheld her former love for the first time in over a decade.

Then she felt the full force of his attention as his gaze settled wholly and purposely on her. Heat danced along her skin. Her pulse sped.

He started toward them, and she felt utterly torn. Part of her wanted to flee. Another part of her wanted to rush to meet him. The largest part of her wanted to stand firmly and call him out for his reprehensible behavior ten years ago.

She opted for the latter. Rather, part of the latter. Or maybe it was really that she couldn't seem to move beneath the weight of his stare. Blast, she hoped it wasn't that, and yet feared that was precisely the case.

He came to a stop next to Poppy. "Good evening." His voice, so deep and silky, like rich, plush velvet, glided over her, eliciting an almost physical response. She felt as though she might sway toward him, her body reacting to his familiarity. But no, he wasn't familiar. This man was a stranger.

She noted the changes in his appearance. His shoulders seemed even broader, if that were possible. His face was more stark as evidenced by the lines around his mouth and the stern set of his jaw. He looked like a man who rarely smiled. The black of his evening clothes gleamed with importance and wealth beneath the flickering chandeliers. He looked every bit a duke and nothing like the young man who'd chased her across a meadow, his dark hair falling across his forehead as he laughed when he caught her.

Poppy turned toward him. "Good evening."

Felicity dropped into another, deeper, curtsey and then assisted her mother in doing the same. "Your Grace, I was just telling your sisters how I looked forward to seeing you." Again, politeness seemed to have taken over her tongue.

"Did you? How surprising after all this time." Calder sounded every bit as cold as she'd imagined him to be given the way he'd rejected her, not at all the young man she'd actually known.

"Yes, it's been many years. I do hope we'll find time to visit." Felicity allowed a bit of sauce into her tone. "If you'll excuse me, I need to see my mother to a chair."

Calder looked at her mother, and for a brief moment, Felicity thought he meant to say something to her—something obnoxious. Before she could think of how to respond if he did, Buckleigh moved toward them, presenting his arm to Felicity's mother. "Allow me to help."

"Thank you, Lord Buckleigh," Mama said, taking his arm.

"I'll be right there, Mama." Felicity watched as they walked away, then looked back to Calder.

"Why are you here?" he asked her sharply, his voice low, but she feared at least Poppy and Bianca could hear.

How dare he question her like that in public? Felicity stiffened. "Everyone comes to the assembly."

"Not here at the assembly, here in *Hartwell*." The outer edge of his lip curled slightly.

"My mother returned to Hartwell last year, and several weeks ago, she became ill. I came to take care of her." Why did she feel so defensive? She didn't have to explain herself to him. On the contrary, if anyone was owed an explanation, it was her.

"So your visit is temporary." There was a hopeful edge to his tone.

It seemed he would like her to say yes. So she said, "I haven't yet decided." She sent a smile toward his sisters, making it clear the expression was for them and not him. "I'm especially glad to be here for the holidays. No one celebrates better than the people of Hartwell." Schooling her features into a mask of concern, she shifted her gaze back to Calder. "I am looking forward to St. Stephen's Day, but I was sad to hear Hartwood would not be hosting the event. I'd feared you were ill." She couldn't think of why else he wouldn't be hosting it. The dukes of Hartwell had done so for generations.

"I am not, as you can see.":

Since he'd decided to speak plainly, so would she. "You don't appear to be, and yet you aren't *quite* the man I remember." Felicity shook her head. She supposed she'd hoped there was a good reason for his rejection ten years ago. A part of her hoped he'd gone on to be happy. She had—as well as she could. She'd loved her husband, but it hadn't ever been the same as what she'd felt for Calder. In fact, she often wondered if their time together had been a dream, that her recollections were somehow a delusion. "But then it's been over a decade."

"Yes, people change over time. And some people change overnight." Calder's eyes burned with a cavalier intensity. "I'm not sure the woman I remember ever existed."

Felicity stared at him, her insides stalling as if she were turning to stone. What was he going on about? That was what she would have said about him.

Poppy reached for her brother's arm. "Calder, perhaps we should—"

He snapped his gaze toward her. "Don't touch me. I will say what I like."

"Not to my wife, you won't." Poppy's husband, the Marquess of Darlington—at least that was who Felicity believed him to be given that he'd referred to Poppy as his wife—stepped between brother and sister.

Poppy seemed surprised to see the marquess but quickly recovered. She glanced about, whispering, "Calder, you're causing a scene."

Calder's gaze darkened, and the marquess took an infinitesimal step toward him. "Careful, Chill, don't let this scene escalate into something else."

What would happen? More importantly, what had become of Calder? For the first time, Felicity felt something she never imagined feeling toward him—concern and maybe a flash of pity.

Calder glared at all of them before settling a particularly horrid stare on Felicity. "I've come to see what I needed to. And now I am free."

He turned abruptly and stalked from the assembly. Felicity snapped her jaw closed before she could gape after him, her mind and body coursing with agitation. What had just occurred?

Darlington turned to Poppy. "I didn't mean to drive him away."

"It was for the best," she murmured.

He offered her his arm. "Shall we take a turn?"

Felicity barely acknowledged that they'd left as she worked to understand why Calder had behaved in such a fashion. He'd said the woman he knew had never existed. She tried to recall the letter he'd written her, words she'd once committed to memory but had since wiped from her mind.

He'd said he wouldn't be courting her or proposing marriage as they'd discussed. He'd said his duty required him to find a more suitable wife. As the daughter of a farmer, she'd feared they had no future, but he'd assured her endlessly that he intended to make her his wife.

Until he'd written the letter and failed to come home for Christmas.

That was when she'd realized it had all been a lie.

CHAPTER 2

"*J*'m sorry about that," Bianca said quietly.

Felicity tried to make sense of Calder's behavior just as she tried to reconcile the blissful time they'd spent together followed by his complete dismissal. It had been more than a lie. It had been a betrayal. And for what? A handful of stolen kisses?

Buckleigh returned from escorting Felicity's mother to the seating area. "Your mother is situated with a few friends." He looked to his wife. "Everything all right?"

"I don't know." She addressed Felicity. "Are *you* all right?"

Felicity mentally shook herself. People were conversing once more, but she was still aware of inquisitive looks drifting in her direction. She blinked and looked at Bianca. "Yes, thank you for your concern. Your brother disturbed me a bit, but I'm fine." She smiled to mask her remaining unease.

Bianca's eyes narrowed. "He's a cad. He didn't even come to my wedding last week."

Felicity was shocked to hear it—in their youth,

he'd always spoken highly of his sisters. "You're joking."

"I wish I were." Bianca exchanged an expression of disappointment and frustration with her husband, though the earl also looked...angry. Felicity could understand that. She was angry too. But she was also baffled. It would be easy to simply walk away and return to York. Why then did she want to find out why Calder held her in such disregard?

Because then she could stop wondering what had happened, what she'd done to drive him away from her. Perhaps her comment that she would pay him a call wasn't merely courtesy. Beyond his behavior toward her—now and in the past—she was curious as to why he wasn't continuing Hartwood's holiday tradition. "Why won't he host the St. Stephen's Day party?"

Bianca scoffed. "He doesn't really have a reason except to imply he can't afford it."

Felicity heard the skepticism in Bianca's voice. "You don't believe that's true?"

Bianca shook her head. "I don't, especially since he kept the money my father left for my dowry."

Felicity gasped, then abruptly lowered her voice lest she draw further attention to them. "Why would he do that?"

"Because he doesn't like me," Buckleigh said. "He refused to give his permission for us to wed."

"Not that I need it." Bianca glowered toward the door as if Calder were still there.

Buckleigh gave her a sympathetic smile. "You did if you wanted your settlement."

"It would have been nice to have so that we could help Hartwell House, not to mention the rebuilding of Shield's End." Bianca referred to the Institution for Impoverished Women and Buckleigh's home. Rather, his home before he'd become the earl of Buckleigh. His seat, Buck Manor, was several miles from Hartwell.

Felicity turned her attention to the earl. "Oh my goodness, I meant to tell you straightaway how sorry I was to hear of the fire. I'm afraid Cal—His Grace—distracted me." She prayed they didn't notice that she'd almost called him by his given name. However, given the flash of surprised interest in Bianca's blue eyes, Felicity was fairly certain at least she had.

"Thank you," Buckleigh responded. "The bright spot in all of it is that we will rebuild Shield's End as the new Institution for Impoverished Women."

"Will you?" Felicity asked. "How marvelous. What will happen to Hartwell House?" The Armstrongs had started the institution for women, particularly those with children, several years ago. Mr. Armstrong had passed away, but his wife continued their work, and everyone in Hartwell supported the endeavor as a benevolent alternative to a workhouse, which would separate the women from their children.

Bianca frowned. "It's in grave disrepair, unfortunately. That is why—well, one of the reasons why—I'm so frustrated with Calder. He refuses to continue the support our father provided to Hartwell House, much to their detriment."

Calder was much worse than Felicity could ever have imagined. It wasn't just that he'd turned cold to her ten years ago, it sounded as if he had no sympathy or concern for others at all. Had she completely misinterpreted the young man she'd fallen in love with, or had he changed that much?

"So he won't support Hartwell House, and he won't host the St. Stephen's Day party." And he'd failed to support his sister or allow her to take control of the settlement her father left for her. Felicity was torn between anger and despair. What had happened to make him so awful?

"That's about right," Bianca said with an exasperated sigh. "I won't get into how awful he is to spend time with. I think you probably gathered that on your own." Bianca winced as she looked at Felicity. "My apologies. I shouldn't speak so freely, but I know you and Calder were once… Never mind. It's none of my business."

Felicity couldn't deny that she'd cared about him. Even after his rejection, she'd hoped he would find happiness as she had with James Garland. It seemed he hadn't. Beyond remaining unwed, he seemed to have distanced himself from everyone and everything that might bring him joy.

Bianca turned to her husband. "Ash, will you give me and Mrs. Garland a moment alone?"

Buckleigh smiled warmly, the love he felt for her evident in his gaze. "Of course. I'll go check on Mrs. Templeton."

"Thank you, my lord," Felicity said.

"Please, call me Ash. I'm afraid I'm still not used to being a lord, and I'm not sure I ever will be—especially among my friends."

Felicity nodded. "You—and you," she said to Bianca, "must call me Felicity. We've all known each other far too long to stand on propriety."

Bianca laughed softly. "I knew there was a reason I liked you so much. My brother is an idiot."

Felicity couldn't disagree with her there. She watched as Ash joined her mother and a couple of other ladies. Bianca linked her arm through Felicity's as the music started.

"Oh dear, I'm keeping you from dancing," Felicity said.

Bianca walked with her to a quieter spot near the wall. "There will be plenty of time for that. I wanted to ask if you had any insight as to why Calder is the way he is."

"Why would I? I haven't seen or communicated with him in over a decade."

"Right." Bianca exhaled. "Poppy and I had a theory that his change in behavior was somehow due to you and whatever happened ten years ago. I suppose we were looking for an easy explanation that would help us understand—and maybe even bring him back."

Was she suggesting that Felicity could fix him? Or that she would at least have the key to doing so? "I'm sorry I can't help you. I'm as perplexed by him as you are. He is not how I remember." At least not until he'd written her that horrid letter.

"I'm so angry, but I'm even more sad." Bianca withdrew her arm from Felicity's. "I want the brother I remember. I just fear he's gone forever." She said the last with such soft despair that Felicity's heart squeezed.

Felicity really didn't think she could help, but would it hurt to try? He clearly held ill will toward her—for a reason she didn't understand. At the very least, she should get to the bottom of that. "I'll pay him a call."

Bianca's eyes widened briefly, and she blinked. "You will?"

"On Monday. Perhaps I can convince him to change his mind about St. Stephen's Day. It's just not right that the Duke of Hartwell doesn't host it."

"Good luck." Bianca's response was heavy with doubt. "Viscount Thornaby has agreed to host the event. We were going to hold it at Shield's End until Thornaby and his cronies set it on fire."

"What?" The word exploded from Felicity. She modulated her tone. "They set it afire?"

"Not on purpose, but they were stupid. They

wanted to play a prank on Ash and set the house ablaze by mistake. To their minimal credit, they are paying for the reconstruction, and Thornaby is falling all over himself to help however he can, including hosting St. Stephen's Day."

"But Thornhill is, what, five miles away? That's an awfully long way for the villagers to travel."

"Yes, but Thornaby and others, including us and Poppy and Gabriel, will provide transportation. It's not ideal, but it's the best we can do in the face of Calder's refusal to hold the party."

"What of the people at Hartwood?" Felicity hated thinking of the estate's tenants and retainers not being able to celebrate a day that had always been specifically about them and their families.

"We'll transport the tenants, but I don't know about the retainers." Bianca's brow furrowed. "I should speak to Truro about that."

Felicity recalled that Truro was the butler. "I'll ask your brother about it when I call."

"Are you sure you want to subject yourself to his rudeness?" Bianca asked.

"I'm not afraid of him." Felicity squared her shoulders. She was suddenly eager for a fight. He'd broken her heart, and she was finally going to call him out for it. "This has been a long time coming."

"You're a brave woman," Bianca said with a chuckle. "I'm not afraid of him either. He's disagreeable and frigid, but he isn't abusive. And he certainly isn't violent."

That was good to know. While Felicity had a hard time reconciling this Calder with the one she'd originally known, she really couldn't imagine him raising a hand to anyone.

"I do hope you'll let us—me and Poppy—know how your visit goes."

Felicity nodded. "Certainly. Now, if you'll excuse me, I should check on my mother."

"Of course. I'll go with you." Bianca smiled, and they linked arms before crossing back to the seating area.

Determination—and a perverse anticipation—curled through Felicity as she contemplated her visit to Hartwood on Monday. She had a litany of things she wanted to say and ask. Perhaps she should make a list…

At last, the time for reckoning was at hand.

~

The bottle of gin on the sideboard in Calder's study beckoned him. Perhaps tonight he would down the contents so that he could find sleep, which had eluded him the past two nights since the assembly.

Since he'd seen Felicity up close.

He closed his eyes and leaned his head back against the chair and greedily devoured the image in his mind. She was even more beautiful than he remembered. The planes of her classically beautiful face were a bit more angular, as if honed by the experiences she'd lived during the years since he'd seen her. Her eyes were still a dark, sparkling green, almost jewellike in their intensity. Her blonde hair looked as silken as ever, styled atop her head and dressed with a pearl comb. The Egyptian-blue dress accentuated the curve of her breast and the dip of her waist. He'd been glad to see she didn't wear widow's colors, as so many women did for years after their husband's demise. Did that mean she wasn't sad?

He opened his eyes, cross with himself for trying to discern her feelings. No, for caring about them. She was a greedy, selfish opportunist. She deserved nothing but his undying contempt.

A knock on the door saved Calder from his aggravating thoughts. "Come," he called as he busied himself with the papers on his desk.

The door pushed halfway open, and Truro, his butler, stepped inside. "You've a visitor, Your Grace."

"Who?" Probably one or both of his sisters. They were the only people who dared come to see him anymore. One day, they would stop. He ignored a flash of unease.

"Mrs. Garland. She's awaiting you in the drawing room."

"I'm busy." But Calder's blood rushed, causing a cacophony in his ears. His heart beat so hard, he feared Truro would hear it.

"I did try to tell her that, but she was most insistent." Truro stated this matter-of-factly and without any concern. He was the only retainer who didn't seem to be intimidated by his employer. Calder wasn't sure how he felt about that. While intimidation wasn't his objective, he appreciated the wide berth everyone cut him.

"Fine." Calder stood and took a deep breath. But his pulse still continued its wild race.

"Shall I bring refreshments?" Truro asked as he moved out of the study.

Calder glowered in response before striding past him toward the drawing room.

With high gilt-edged ceilings and an imposing portrait of his father over the fireplace, the drawing room was intended to be the most luxurious room at Hartwood. Calder hadn't changed a thing since his father had died. It wasn't that he didn't want to—he despised everything his father liked, and the man had loved this room. However,

Calder's commitment to frugality was greater than his desire to destroy everything his father had cared about. His father would have expected him to "waste money" refurbishing the room, and so he hadn't.

Pausing at the threshold, Calder's gaze moved immediately to Felicity. She stood before the windows that overlooked the gardens and parkland beyond. Her form and profile looked regal in her dark green velvet costume. A jaunty cream-colored feather curled up from her hat, irritating him. She shouldn't look so fresh and lovely.

"I can't credit why you would come here," he said as he stalked into the center of the room. He realized he did want to intimidate *her*. Maybe because his heart was still crashing as if it wanted to escape his body.

She turned from the window, a half smile arresting her mouth. Her gaze raked over him slowly before settling on his face.

He couldn't tell what she thought of her perusal. That irritated him too.

"Good afternoon, Your Grace."

"If you came for a pleasant conversation to catch up on the past ten years, you will be sorely disappointed."

"I did not," she said softly, walking toward him but stopping a few feet away.

In addition to her hat, she was also still wearing her gloves. Clearly, she didn't mean to stay. Good.

"I came to discuss the St. Stephen's Day party."

He grunted. "My sisters sent you."

"Bianca and I discussed it, but I wanted to come." Now her lips curled into a full smile, but it wasn't the kind that held joy. It was the kind a predator unfurled just before moving to strike its prey.

Calder was no one's prey. "You've made a grave mistake."

She lifted her shoulder in a thoroughly elegant fashion. "Probably, but I'm here nonetheless. Before we discuss the party—and I mean to before I leave—I think we should perhaps clear the air between us. You are angry with me, but I can't fathom why."

She sounded so calm, so reasonable. He almost believed she had no idea. "Have you forgotten what you did? I can't see how that's possible given how drastically it changed your life."

Her eyes narrowed in confusion. "What *I* did?"

He wanted to laugh, but there was nothing humorous about the situation. In fact, he found her attempts at forgetting the past infuriating. "You left."

"*I*...left?" She shook her head. "You didn't come home for Christmas."

"Why would I, knowing that you'd gotten what you wanted and fled?"

She took a step toward him, her eyes dark, the muscles of her jaw tense. "I didn't get what I wanted at all. All I wanted was you." Her words sliced through him, arousing the pain he'd thought long buried. "But you said I wasn't good enough, that you couldn't make me your duchess."

No, that wasn't what had happened at all. His mind raced back to that time, to the visit his father had paid him in Scotland, where Calder had gone to spend the fall at a friend's hunting lodge. The news he'd delivered ricocheted through Calder's brain.

His father had met him in the gathering room of the lodge, his expression foreboding. *"I know you'll think poorly of me, but this is a case in which the ends thoroughly justified the means."* Calder couldn't have begun to imagine what he'd said next. *"I offered Miss Templeton and her family a great sum of money to leave Hartwell. She was more than eager to accept. She never wanted you, just your title and, more importantly, money. I didn't even have to convince her —she was relieved to be free of any promises she made you."*

Calder responded to her, his voice eerily quiet and strange to his own ears. "I *never* said that. Do you deny your family took money from my father and left Hartwell?"

"Money? No!" She set her hands on her hips, her eyes blazing with anger. "We left Hartwell because my father thought I would want to be away from you. He sold his farm, and we moved to York, where my brother lived."

She had to be lying. Calder had no other explanation.

Except he did. His father hadn't been pleased to learn that Calder wished to court Felicity. But then his father had rarely been pleased with anything Calder did.

He managed to find his voice—barely. "My father said he offered you money to leave and that you gleefully accepted it, that you were glad to be free of me."

Her face went pale, and Calder wondered if she might faint. Then he saw her shoulders stiffen. "I did no such thing, nor did your father offer me anything save a letter from you that said you had no desire to marry me, that I was not an appropriate wife for a duke."

Calder felt light, as if he were floating, as if the earth beneath him had been jerked away. "I didn't write you a letter."

She moved closer, her hand stretching toward him. "Are you all right?"

He stepped back, out of her reach. "I'm fine." But he wasn't. Everything he'd believed for the past decade had been a lie. His father had driven a wedge between him and Felicity. No, not a wedge. He'd burned their dreams to the ground.

And Felicity had wed someone else while Calder had gone to London and raised merry hell until he'd lost everything but the clothes he was wearing and the set of emerald jewelry his mother had left him. The necklace, earrings, and ring had been intended for his wife. Instead, he'd sold them and used them to rebuild himself without a drop of help from his father.

"Well, *I'm* not fine," Felicity said, her brow creased and her mouth turning down. She crossed her arms over her chest, looking bereft. "I thought you didn't want me. To know you did…"

"Don't." Calder couldn't follow that path. That was the distant past. He was not the same man who'd been easily manipulated. "We can't change what happened." And to even think about it would welcome a barrage of hurt he didn't think he could manage. Nor did he want to.

"You can simply forget about it?" She blinked at him, then stared into his eyes for a long, uncomfortable moment. "We can't change the past, but knowing the truth changes everything."

"It doesn't." It couldn't. He refused to open himself up to…anything. "I need to get back to work." He started to turn, but she came forward and clasped his arm.

Though she wore gloves and the layers of his clothes separated her touch from his flesh, he felt the connection down to the very marrow of his bones. The sensation sizzled through him, reawakening a yearning he hadn't felt in forever.

Or, more accurately, in ten years.

He pulled his arm from her grasp and stared at her hand. She dropped it to her side and looked up at him. "I told you I wasn't leaving until we talked about St. Stephen's Day."

She had said that, dammit. "There's nothing to discuss. Thornaby is hosting it this year."

"Why aren't you?"

Because his father had loved it. Everyone believed St. Stephen's Day was for the retainers and the villagers, that it was their favorite day of the year. While all that might be true, Calder's father had loved it most of all. Everyone heralded him as some sort of king, a benevolent being who deigned to give his people a day of rest and celebration. Everything he did was designed to earn himself praise and adoration. And it worked for everyone, including Calder's sisters.

"It's an expensive event." Even if the cost wasn't his primary reason for refusing to host the party, the statement wasn't a lie.

Her blonde brows arched briefly. "I'm sure you can afford it."

"You know nothing about my finances, nor should you presume." He *could* afford it, but after losing everything and amassing a fortune entirely on his own, he was loath to let any of it go. And the truth was that his father, despite his claims to the contrary, had been a poor financial manager. There was money, but not as much as there should have been. Calder planned to make the dukedom more financially secure than ever before.

"I beg your pardon," she said, but he caught a note of exasperation in her voice. "What if others supported the cost and you merely allowed the event to take place here? It would ease the burden of transporting everyone to Thornhill."

"That isn't my concern."

She blew out a frustrated breath, her brows pitching low over her magnificent eyes. "Of course it is. St. Stephen's Day has been the concern of the dukes of Hartwell for generations."

"Not anymore."

She cocked her head to the side, her expression both curious and pleading. "Why? What has changed?"

"I am the duke now. There is no law saying I must host anything." He narrowed his eyes at her, irritated that she would question him, but also perversely enjoying their exchange. What the hell was wrong with him? "Even if there was, I'm the magistrate."

"So you'd break the law to suit yourself?"

"I *am* the law. However, in this case, there is no law, only your expectation."

She sucked in a sharp breath, and for the first time, he saw something in her eyes he didn't like: pity. Just like that, any pleasure he'd found—and it had been the first in some time—evaporated. "Are you like this because of me? Rather, because of what your father did?"

A thousand emotions exploded inside him, none of which he wanted to address. He was done with this interview. "You've done what you came to do. We've settled the past and we've discussed St. Stephen's Day. I believe we are finished with each other."

His statement sounded final, and he'd meant it to. With the slight narrowing of her gaze and tightening of her jaw, he wasn't sure she agreed.

"You've yet to provide an acceptable reason for not hosting the party. You don't have to pay for anything."

"It would be an inconvenience. Just as you are being right now."

Her jaw dropped open for a moment before she snapped it shut and pursed her lips. "You bear absolutely no resemblance to the Calder I knew."

Her use of his name was both a balm and a friction. He didn't want either. "Because that man doesn't exist anymore. I'll have Truro show you out." He turned on his heel and quit the drawing room, his heart pounding nearly as hard as when he'd arrived.

"Bloody hell," he swore as he returned to his study. Running his hand through his hair, he tried to banish the encounter from his mind. But all he could see was her heart-shaped face with its stunning—and provocative—emerald eyes. All he could feel was the touch of her hand on his sleeve. All he could smell was the faint scent of bergamot and roses.

Memories he'd worked too hard to bury rose in his mind—holding her hand, laughing with her, taking her lips in the sweetest of kisses…

He'd spent the last decade in some sort of purgatory. Now he feared he would spend the next in hell.

CHAPTER 3

*T*he butler came into the drawing room a moment later. Or perhaps it was longer. Felicity was not terribly aware of the passage of time, not when she'd fallen into a state of absolute numbness.

"Mrs. Garland?" Truro prompted softly from just inside the doorway.

Felicity shook her head and brought herself to the present. If she didn't, she was going to completely lose herself in the past—a past that had stolen her future.

Bitterness stole her breath for a moment. She lifted her hand to her chest and blinked, lest she dissolve into a puddle of tears in front of Calder's butler.

But she wasn't a crier. She was made of stiff, strong stuff, or so her father said.

Her father. Had he played some part in Calder's father's nefarious scheme? Had Calder's father settled some amount of money on them so they could move to York? In hindsight, it was odd how quickly he'd decided to relocate and the ease with which he'd sold the farm.

Her breath caught again, but tears didn't

threaten this time. She felt a wave of outrage. However, there was no one to whom she could direct the emotion.

"Mrs. Garland?" the butler repeated.

"My apologies," she said hastily. "I don't suppose you would tell me where I might find His Grace?"

Truro gave her an apologetic look, his features briefly flinching. "I don't think that's wise."

"Probably not. However, I must speak with him for just another moment. If you don't tell me, I shall go in search of him." She gave him a sly look. "Will you stop me?"

He straightened, and there was a tinge of something in his gaze—admiration, perhaps. "I will not." He lowered his voice to nearly a whisper. "His study is in the northeast corner."

"Bless you, Truro." She flashed him a smile before hurrying from the room.

Good heavens, what was she doing? Calder didn't want to see her. He'd barely stomached their conversation in the drawing room. He also seemed utterly unmovable about St. Stephen's Day.

And yet there was something inside him—something she'd glimpsed when she'd asked if his father had caused him to be the way he was now. Thinking back, Calder hadn't spoken to her much of his father. Now that she knew the man had orchestrated the destruction of their almost-courtship, she wondered how else he'd influenced Calder. What didn't she know?

Probably nothing he would tell her.

Still, she was going to try. She'd loved him ten years ago, and he'd loved her. Through no fault of theirs, save their naïve idiocy in believing the lies his father had spun, they'd been robbed of their chance together. *Then.*

Now, they had another chance. Felicity didn't mean to waste it.

She found his study with ease. However, the door was closed. Standing outside, she chewed her lip. She ought to knock, but she was rather past following propriety.

Before she could talk herself out of it, she opened the door and strode inside. Calder turned from the sideboard on the right side of the room. A fire crackled in the hearth on the left wall, a chair angled nearby to welcome the heat. His desk, stacked neatly with a ledger and the post, stood before a wide set of windows.

She took all that in very briefly before settling her gaze on her prey. "You seem as if you need a friend. I should like to put myself forward for the position."

He stared at her, his mouth dropping open. He clacked his teeth together. "I do not need a friend, and if I did, it wouldn't be you."

"Why not? We were great friends, I think. More than friends, but we don't have to discuss that. I realize a great deal of time has passed." Her heart squeezed. So much lost time. Yet, she couldn't discount it—she'd been fond of her husband and the years they'd spent together. It had been precisely the type of marriage her mother had encouraged her to embark upon. Their union had been based on mutual respect and shared interests. Mama had said love would come in time, as it had between her and Papa, but Felicity had never truly felt that emotion for James—at least not in the way that she'd felt it for Calder.

Oh, Calder. Her heart ached to see him standing before her, his face drawn, his entire demeanor radiating a seemingly impenetrable cold aloofness.

"An eternity has passed," Calder said. "How did

you find me? Am I going to have to terminate Truro's employment?"

"Absolutely not. I told him I was leaving, but I looked for you instead."

"What joy." He poured himself a glass of brandy.

Was that sarcasm? That was far better than abject frigidity!

She eyed the glass in his hand. "You aren't going to offer me any?"

"No. I want you to leave."

"I will if you promise me something."

He snorted, then took a swig of his brandy. He arched a brow at her, and her heart skipped. That was more like the Calder she'd known. And loved.

"Promise me you'll *think* about allowing us to host the St. Stephen's Day celebration here."

"Fine."

She would wager her house in York he was lying. "Excellent. I'll return tomorrow so we can discuss it again." In the meantime, she'd visit Bianca and ensure there were adequate funds to support the event without asking Calder to contribute.

He frowned deeply, his entire face contorting so that she nearly laughed. "Please don't."

"Then you can visit me. I'm staying with my mother in Hartwell. She's leasing Ivy Cottage."

"No."

"Then I'll come here."

"You're incredibly persistent. Even worse than Bianca."

"That is quite a compliment, thank you. I will continue to persist until you agree. I've nothing better to do, you see."

"I do," he said sourly before drinking more brandy.

"You see, or you have something better to do?"

He scowled at her. "Both. Do not visit me tomorrow. I will consider your request and let you know by...Thursday."

"It would be better to know sooner so that we can change the arrangements." She flashed him her most winning smile.

"You actually think I'm going to change my mind."

"If I didn't, I would give up now. I'll come back on Wednesday, all right?" She didn't wait for him to respond. "I also want you to reconsider your support of Hartwell House. I understand the building is in disrepair and you've ceased the support your father" —she allowed her lip to curl slightly—"gave the institution."

How had the man been so kindhearted when it came to charitable endeavors and his tenants and retainers, and yet absolutely diabolical regarding his son's heart? She longed to ask Calder about that and hoped she'd have the chance. Her persistence wasn't going to be limited to St. Stephen's Day or Hartwell House... She was going to do more than save a holiday and a local institution—she was going to save him too.

His gray gaze darkened like a storm cloud bursting with rain. "Now, you're treading too far. Actually, you've been doing that since you arrived. Be gone with you."

She gave him a pointed stare. "I shall persist." Then she turned and left before he could say anything further.

That had gone better than she'd thought. She'd half expected him to rail at her and banish her from the estate forever. Instead, she'd secured a future appointment with him, even if he didn't really want it.

As her coach rambled from the estate, her bravado faltered. A sense of melancholy settled over her. No, it was something far deeper—a soul-deep sadness over a love not lost, but stolen. There was anger, despair, regret, and just a crushing… grief. She realized a tear had escaped her eye and now made its way down her cheek.

If this was how she was feeling, she could only imagine Calder's response. He was already so broken—at least that was how he appeared to her. Learning that his father had lied about buying her off had to be a staggering blow.

If he hadn't needed saving before, she would say he did now. And she would be the one to do it —whether he wanted her to or not.

~

*T*he sun was bright against the backs of his eyelids and warm upon his face. The grass was soft beneath him, the smell of honeysuckle rife in the air as the breeze tickled his nose.

"Are you asleep?"

The soft, sweet voice of his love was even more beautiful than the summer day. He opened his eyes and saw her leaning over him. Tendrils of her blonde hair grazed her cheeks, and the sun behind her created a halo around her head.

"You look like an angel," he whispered.

"Then you are surely the devil." She waggled her brows at him, then laughed softly.

"Temptress," he muttered before curling his hand around her neck and pulling her down to kiss him.

Their lips met with a spark of heat and desire. Longing swept through him. It was torture to kiss her like this knowing he couldn't do more. He wouldn't—not until they were wed.

He opened his mouth, and she did the same, their tongues meeting in a clash of hunger and exploration.

With his other hand, he clasped her hip, pulling her down on top of him.

She pressed against him, bringing their bodies flush. He groaned, basking in the pure delight of her embrace and this perfect, blissful afternoon. If only it could always be like this... When they wed, it would be. After he returned from Scotland, he'd court her over the Christmas holidays, and they would marry after Epiphany. The future had never looked so wonderful.

He flipped her over to her back, provoking her to gasp into his mouth and then giggle. He pulled back long enough to grin at her. Then the ground began to move.

The blades of grass grew and wound themselves around her, claiming her body as the dirt beneath her gave way. Her green eyes grew wide. She fell away from him, slowly, pulled by the grass and dirt. He couldn't hold her. Terror seized his heart, and he called her name. Over and over.

"Don't let me go!" she cried. "You promised we'd be together."

"Never." The voice of his father boomed all around him like thunder. The sun disappeared, taking its light and warmth. The earth turned gray and barren.

Then the ground swallowed her whole, and he lay facedown in the grass. Only it wasn't grass anymore. It was a carpet pressing into his face.

"You're pathetic." His father again.

Calder blinked as his apartment at the Albany came into view.

"I'm not giving you any more money," the duke spat. "You are on your own. What an embarrassment to me, to our family."

Calder's stomach roiled. "I'm not," he murmured, his voice failing to carry any volume.

"Pull yourself together and come see me. I'll put you on a mail coach to County Durham."

Home...Hartwell...where she'd chosen money over him. He'd never go back.

"No," Calder croaked, lifting his head from the floor and squinting up at the murky figure standing over him.

The tip of a boot crashed against Calder's rib. "Then you are on your own."

Calder dropped his head, but it wasn't a floor. It was soft, like a pillow...

Gasping, Calder turned over and sat up, his chest heaving. Sweat dripped from his forehead as the bedclothes fell away from his upper body. He drew in deep breaths, trying to shake the grip of the nightmare.

It was just a dream.

Except those things had happened. They were memories—the joyous afternoon with Felicity, his father's cold callousness.

However, now he was viewing them with a different perspective. His father had been even more cruel than Calder had known. His expectations and demands—his abuse—had been bad enough, but now Calder knew what he'd actually done. His father had used malicious deception to separate him from the woman he loved. She'd never taken money from him.

Or so she said.

Calder wiped a hand across his dewy brow. He'd spent ten years hating her, and now he was simply going to take what she said as truth?

The alternative was to believe his father's version of what had happened. Ten years ago, he would have believed her without question. Now... now he was bitter and distrustful, and he guarded himself from everyone and everything.

His heart had slowed, and as the sweat dappling his skin began to evaporate, he became cold. The coals smoldered in the fireplace grate, visible through a gap in the curtain surrounding his bed. Scowling, he lay back and pulled the covers up to his chin.

The truth didn't matter. What had happened a decade ago was in the past, and they couldn't change any of it. He'd dug himself out of despair and failure, and with his father's death, he would build a new legacy for the dukedom. His father had wanted him to be ruthless in his endeavors, whether it was school, marriage, or finances. He'd demanded Calder be the best in everything—there was no time for love or softheartedness. That could all come later, when he'd done all he needed to do to establish himself as a premier nobleman of the realm. Each duke owed it to their heritage to climb higher than the last.

Calder was doing just that. His fortune was greater, his holdings more vast, his influence without compare. Now would be the time he should take a wife and support the local community—things his father would have demanded he do if he were here.

But he wasn't, and Calder would do the exact opposite. His father would be horrified to learn that Calder would never wed or provide an heir, that he refused to support Hartwell House, that he'd put an end to hundreds of years of tradition.

And that made Calder happy.

Well, as happy as Calder would ever be. That wasn't an emotion he recognized anymore.

But there'd been a flicker that afternoon...when Felicity had visited...

Why the hell had he agreed to consider allowing the St. Stephen's Day party to be held here? And why had he consented to her paying *another* visit that would only upend his carefully wrought façade?

She also wanted him to rethink his decision to no longer support Hartwell House. But he wasn't a hero—not for her, not for anyone. The sooner she accepted that, the better off they would all be.

He'd had a thought about Hartwell House, which he'd mentioned to his sisters. It was time to make that thought a reality. Hartwell House ought to be a workhouse. If they wanted to rebuild Buckleigh's property, Shield's End, as a new institution, it should be as a workhouse operated by the county. Coddling people never did any good—his father had been right about that at least.

Calder closed his eyes and hoped his sleep would not be troubled further. He worked hard to keep memories from surfacing in his mind. Learning what he had today didn't change that. The past needed to stay where it belonged: in the past.

CHAPTER 4

"Good morning, Mrs. Garland," Agatha, their maid of all work, greeted Felicity with a pleasant smile.

Tired due to a rather restless night, Felicity stifled a yawn as she stepped off the last stair. "Good morning, Agatha. Is my mother up?"

"Yes, she just sat down at the table. I am fetching breakfast."

"Thank you." Felicity inclined her head, and the woman, who was about ten years Felicity's senior and lived right outside the center of Hartwell with her husband and son, took herself off toward the small kitchen at the back of the cottage.

Felicity moved toward the parlor where they took breakfast at a two-person round table situated near the window that overlooked the street. She hesitated at the doorway. As Agatha had indicated, Mama was already seated.

After spending the night consumed with thoughts of Calder and the years they'd lost, Felicity was as exhausted in mind as she was in body. Despite that, she knew she must summon the courage to speak to her mother about what she'd learned the day before.

Felicity hadn't been able to broach the subject when she'd returned yesterday. She'd been too overwhelmed with the new knowledge—and with spending time with Calder.

Her heart soared when she thought of him, but only for a moment before the weight of his coldness crushed it down. And then she felt as if she could bleed for him.

"Felicity?" Mama called from the table. Her brow creased as she regarded Felicity with a perplexed expression. "Did you forget something?"

"No." Felicity gave her head a tiny shake, then went to the table and sat across from her mother, who poured her a cup of tea.

"Did you sleep well?" Mama asked.

"Not particularly." There was no point prevaricating. She needed to clear her mind. "The call I paid yesterday was on His Grace." She didn't have to say which duke. There was only one in the vicinity, and there was really only one, period, so far as Felicity was concerned.

Surprise flickered through Mama's gaze before she plucked a roll from the basket between them. "And how did he receive you?"

"Not well," Felicity said.

Agatha came in with two covered plates and placed one before each of them. Removing the covers, she revealed coddled eggs and ham before telling them to enjoy and leaving.

Felicity picked up her fork but didn't eat. Instead, she continued, eyeing her mother with uncertainty. "He holds me in strong disregard. He believes I accepted money from his father and left Hartwell ten years ago to avoid marrying him. Of course I did no such thing." Her insides swirled with anxiety, but she plowed forward. "I wonder, however, if Papa did? Took money from His Grace, I mean." There, she'd said it.

Mama paused in cutting her ham, her body going stiff. When her eyes met Felicity's, there were tears. "I'm so sorry." The apology was soft and low, and it tore at Felicity's battered heart.

"Oh, Mama." The back of Felicity's throat itched, but she swallowed the sensation. Reaching across the table, she briefly touched her mother's wrist. "Why would he do that?"

Sniffing, Mama set her utensils down, then dabbed at her eyes with her napkin. "Your father had talked of selling the farm—he was tired, and neither of your brothers wanted to take it over. When His Grace offered a large sum of money for the property, Percy leapt at the chance. But there was a condition: we had to leave Hartwell and you were not to wed Chilton." She referred to Calder by his former title. "Your father agreed."

"The duke made certain I wouldn't marry his son." Anger rose inside Felicity. She clutched her hands together in her lap, squeezing her frustration through her fingers. "He forged a letter from Calder saying he didn't want to marry me, that I wasn't good enough. But you know that, of course," she said sadly, recalling how she'd sobbed all over her mother for weeks, even after they'd moved to York.

Mama nodded as she dabbed at a fresh wash of tears. "I wasn't sure if it was a forgery, but it seemed clear His Grace was not in favor of your marriage. He was a very powerful man, Felicity. We took the money and left, just as he wanted."

Felicity wanted to understand, but the pain in her chest was nearly crushing. "I loved him."

"You said you did, but you were too young."

"I'm not too young now. I know my mind—

now and then. I loved him, and he loved me. We lost a decade together."

"But you loved James!" Mama cried. "You had a good marriage."

"Yes, we did, but I didn't love him. I cared for him a great deal. However, it wasn't the same." There was no comparing the affection she'd felt for her twenty-years-older husband to the wild tide of passion she'd possessed for Calder. A passion that had reawakened yesterday. Part of her sleeplessness was due to remembering the way he'd caressed her, kissed her, and looked at her as if she were the most important thing in the entire world. What she wouldn't give to experience all that again.

"Mama, when I think of what I missed, I am angry and sad. However, I can't change the past." Calder had been right about that, at least, even if he was misled in holding on to those feelings of rage and loss. "And neither can you. I forgive you—and Papa." If Felicity had learned anything, especially after spending time with Calder the day before, it was that life was too short to hold grudges or allow hurt to rule your emotions.

Mama clasped her hand over her mouth and nodded as more tears leaked from her eyes. Sniffing loudly, she wiped her face. "I'm so sorry. I honestly don't know what else we could have done." She blanched. "Is His Grace terribly angry?"

Among other things, but Felicity didn't acknowledge that. Whatever he felt, whatever might be between them would be just that—between *them*.

"He's moved on," Felicity said carefully.

"He has a reputation for being cold and cruel. He rarely comes to the village. And he's never wed.

Did we…" Mama shook her head and turned to look out the window, her jaw clenching.

"As I said, we can't change the past. We are here at this moment, and I mean to try to repair things as best as I can."

Mama snapped her gaze back to Felicity, her lips parting as she stared at her a moment. "Are you going to try to pursue a courtship with him again?"

Felicity arched a shoulder. "I don't know if that's possible. However, if I can help him find the joy that seems to be missing from his life, I will consider that a blessing. And it's the least our family owes him."

Nodding, Mama set her napkin back in her lap. "You've a good heart, dear."

Felicity was counting on Calder's being the same—once she cut through the darkness to get there.

By that afternoon, Felicity had listened to her mother apologize dozens of times, and Felicity was more than ready to leave for Buck Manor. The journey was twelve miles, long enough for Felicity to shake off her lingering upset from that morning as well as contemplate her next steps with Calder.

Today, she would speak with Bianca about the St. Stephen's Day party and Hartwell House. Felicity was committed to bringing Calder around on those issues, at least. And if that went well, she'd convince him to apologize to Bianca and give her the settlement he'd denied her.

Goodness, she didn't want much, did she?

It occurred to Felicity—constantly, really—that she'd embarked on a fool's mission. Still, she had to try. Not just for the benefit of the village, the people of the Hartwood estate, and the inhabitants of Hartwell House, but for Calder's very soul. She could see that he was nearly gone, a shell of a man.

Nearly being the key word.

There were glimmers of hope beneath his shell, and Felicity was clinging to those as if her life depended on it. Or his.

When her coach arrived at Buck Manor, she was teeming with energy and anticipation. She was ready to wipe away the last ten years.

The butler took her outer accessories and showed her to the drawing room. Greenery decorated the mantel and windows, and mistletoe hung near the doorway. Bianca didn't keep her waiting long.

"Felicity! How lovely to see you so soon." Bianca strode toward her, a bundle of vivacity wrapped in a forest-green gown. "My goodness, this is quite a journey for you to take by yourself. Your mother didn't come?"

Felicity shook her head. "She's still recuperating, though she probably would have liked to. Even so, this is a visit I needed to make on my own."

Bianca arched a brow, her gaze curious. "I see." She gestured toward a seating area near the hearth, where a warm fire blazed. "Shall we sit?"

Felicity went to the settee while Bianca took a chair angled nearby. "I visited Calder yesterday." She used his name and decided not to censor herself. He would always be Calder to her, and frankly, she didn't care who knew it.

Now both of Bianca's dark brows climbed her forehead. "You actually went?"

Felicity nodded. "He's really a mess, isn't he?"

Bianca laughed. "How lovely to speak with someone about him openly! Besides my sister and Ash, of course. You're very brave to have gone. How did it go?"

"As well as you can imagine. He said he can't afford to host the St. Stephen's Day celebration, but I can't see how that's possible."

"Thank you!" Bianca crowed. "Neither can I."

"I told him that, but it only made him grumpier. So I suggested he let us—you and whoever else, I mean—host the party at Hartwood without an expense to him."

"Hell, why didn't I think of that?" Bianca asked, tapping her finger against her lip.

"Would you be amenable to that arrangement?"

"I would be *thrilled* with that arrangement. Did he actually agree?" Bianca looked incredulous. "You will have worked a miracle."

"Don't give me credit yet. He's thinking about it."

"That's further than I got with him." Bianca leaned back and crossed her arms. "This is an excellent solution and would be so much easier than transporting everyone to Thornhill."

"Hopefully, he will agree." Felicity doubted he would, which meant she had to find a way to convince him. Perhaps she could circumvent him and go straight to Truro for assistance... The butler was a beacon of hope in that household.

Bianca uncrossed her arms and scooted forward, her eyes alight. "He won't, but perhaps we could trick him."

Felicity laughed, amused they had come to, more or less, the same conclusion. "How loyal is Truro to him?"

"Not as loyal as he is to me," Bianca said with devious glee, her eyes narrowing. "Oh, I must think on this. You're calling on him again tomorrow?" At Felicity's nod, she went on. "I suppose it wouldn't be helpful for me to go with you."

"I don't think so." Felicity was counting on having an advantage that only she possessed—their shared history. Which, unfortunately, included heartbreak. Perhaps what she needed to do was give him new memories… "Bianca, will you be able to coordinate moving the party to Hartwood?"

"Certainly. Ash's mother has been helping me." Bianca tipped her head to the side. "Did you also say you spoke to him about Hartwell House?"

"I did, briefly. You said at the assembly that it's in need of repair."

"Yes, several of the rooms leak, and there really isn't enough space to accommodate everyone. The new Shield's End will support the institution in a much better fashion, but that won't be for some time, so Hartwell House must be fixed. Furthermore, we plan to use Hartwell House as a school for the children who live at Hartwell House and as a day school for anyone else in the area."

"That's absolutely marvelous." Felicity felt a sudden urge to move back to Hartwell so she could be a part of these exciting changes.

Or was it so she could be close to Calder?

She wasn't ready to answer that question. Wanting to restore him to a place of peace and happiness wasn't the same as rekindling their relationship. Except she feared she wouldn't get to decide if she wanted that or not. The passion she'd felt for him in their youth had seemed utterly beyond her control or imagination.

"Poppy and Gabriel already do so much for Hartwell House," Bianca said. "And now Ash and I are focused on rebuilding Shield's End. Continuing the support our father gave to Hartwell House is the least Calder can do. Honestly, even if he would just give my dowry settlement to them, I would be grateful."

Felicity inclined her head. "That's very selfless of you."

"It would be if I were allowed to do it." She exhaled in frustration. "They need the money more than we do, more than Calder does, I daresay. I honestly don't know how he became such a miser."

Felicity thought she knew at least part of the story, but suspected there was more. And she was determined to find out.

~

*T*hough Calder was expecting Felicity's call, his heart still pounded when her coach stopped in front of the house. He could see the vehicle from the window of his study, but then, he'd been watching for her the past hour or more.

He stood from his desk and went to the window. He'd dreamed of her again last night, but not in the way he had the night before. That had been a nightmare—because of his father.

Calder shoved thoughts of him away. He'd ruined Calder's life once—maybe twice—and he refused to allow him to do it again.

He watched her alight from the coach and then disappear from view. Turning to the door, he took a deep breath and waited for Truro to come fetch him.

Isis sat in front of the fire, her gaze fixed on him as if she were waiting expectantly too.

After several long minutes, Calder began to pace. What was taking so long? He kept himself from going in search of her. Meanwhile, Isis followed his movements, her eyes never leaving his form.

At last, Truro rapped on the door.

"Come," Calder barked, frowning sharply as he stopped and pivoted toward the door.

Truro opened the door and inclined his head.

"Mrs. Garland is here. She awaits you in the drawing room."

"It's about bloody time," Calder muttered, striding past Truro on his way to the drawing room. At the threshold, he stopped short and stared at the scene before him.

Felicity sat on a blanket spread across the center of the room, the skirt of her bright blue gown arranged around her like the petals of a flower. A basket sat at the edge of the blanket, and plates of food were arranged, along with two tankards.

"Is that ale?" he asked, a long-ago memory rushing to his mind.

"Yes."

"And blackberry scones." His gaze landed on the plate that held the confection.

"Yes."

He knew everything that was on the blanket—it was a recreation of a picnic they'd had ten years ago. On the very day he'd kissed her beneath the blazing sun. The day he'd dreamed about the other night, before it had become a nightmare.

Wariness crept over him, diluting a shocking rush of pleasure. Even the blanket she sat upon looked the same.

"What are you doing?" The question fell from his mouth, a defense against an onslaught of emotion he didn't want.

"Having a picnic. I'm afraid it's too cold outside. I was worried it might snow."

Calder had been worried about that too. In fact, he'd threatened the sky if it dared prevent Felicity from coming. Which meant he'd looked forward to her visit. Not that he would ever admit it aloud.

"Aren't you going to sit?" she asked.

"I'm not hungry." Except he was. For her.

The years had been more than kind to her. She was even more beautiful now than he remembered. Experience gave her features an alluring wisdom. And her stature exuded confidence and grace—things a girl of eighteen didn't always have in great abundance.

Or a young man of twenty.

God, they'd been young. And naïve. And so foolish. To think they could forge a future—the heir to a dukedom and the daughter of a common farmer...

He went to the blanket, drawn by some invisible thread. Or perhaps the lure of what he'd missed.

He dropped down and reached for the tankard, eager for a fortifying drink of ale. "Did you get this from Tom?"

She nodded. "Of course. Where else would I get it?"

Tom was Hartwell's only brewer. "I have my own here."

"Perhaps we should sample it as well," she suggested brightly as she plucked up her tankard. Holding it toward him, she said, "Let us toast to the future."

He didn't want to drink to that. And yet he *needed* a drink to steady his nerves. He didn't tap his tankard to hers but lifted it and took a drink.

She did the same, then set it down before reaching for the plate of scones. "Would you like a scone? My maid, Agatha, made them this morning. She's a magnificent cook."

"I see what you're trying to do," he said.

"And what is that?" she asked innocently.

"This is disturbingly close to a picnic we shared once."

"Is it disturbing? I should hope not. I have fond

memories of that day. In fact, it is among my most favorite recollections."

His pulse racing, he took a long pull on his ale. "Those aren't dedicated to your husband?"

"No," she said softly. "I have lovely memories of our marriage, but they are…not the same."

Something inside Calder unfurled, like a flower blooming beneath the rays of the sun. "I'd heard you were a widow. How did he die?" Calder busied himself with a bite of scone while he awaited her response.

"He was ill for a long time. He was twenty years older than me."

Calder hadn't known that. "You fell in love with him?"

"No. He was kind, and I felt I should marry."

He'd imagined her falling in love with a dashing young man and then pining sorrowfully after losing him. That he'd been utterly wrong was both relieving and…sad. "Were you happy, at least?"

"Yes. He was an excellent husband. We weren't blessed with children, but we had a nice life."

Her description sounded so…pleasant. And while it wasn't what he'd thought their marriage would have been, a "nice life" was still a far cry better than Calder's. "Well, I'm sorry for your loss."

"Thank you." She sipped her ale. "Why haven't you wed?" She eyed him cautiously over the rim of her tankard.

"I've been too busy." He'd completely ignored the Marriage Mart in London. Instead, he'd spent a few years perfecting rakish behavior, conducting liaisons as the mood struck him. The past few years, he'd kept a mistress, but he always terminated the arrangement at the end of the Season. Right now, he couldn't remember any of their names or faces. All he recalled was Felicity. Her winning smile, her gorgeous eyes, her sparkling laugh.

She reached for a fig. "It's good that we're indoors. Do you remember what happened at the picnic?" The edge of her mouth ticked up in a half smile.

For the first time in Calder didn't know how long, he felt his lips tug. How would it feel to smile? To laugh? "You're referring to the bird who defecated on the blanket? Is this the same blanket, by the way?"

She nodded. "You remember." Her tone vibrated with happiness. The sound shot through him like a thousand fireworks exploding in the sky.

He remembered every moment—the bird, their laughter, his scolding of the fowl who had long since disappeared into the beyond. The taste of berries on his tongue, the rush of desire as he'd watched her lick her fingers, the softness of her lips against his.

That she'd kept the blanket and had brought it today stirred a rush of pleasure inside him. He took another drink of ale, completely at odds with himself. This was at once strange and unwanted while feeling utterly familiar and...wonderful.

"I did try to recreate that day," Felicity said softly. "However, I don't have a dog."

Now Calder did laugh. The sensation was odd and surprising, so much so that Calder transformed it into a cough. The sparkle in Felicity's eyes told him she wasn't convinced he was coughing, that she knew he'd laughed. "You remember the dog?" she asked.

He nodded, then whistled. A moment later, Isis trotted into the drawing room. She came and sat down next to Calder.

Felicity smiled warmly at the greyhound. "Who is this beautiful creature?"

"This is Isis." Calder petted her head, and she nuzzled his hand. "Unlike the dog who interrupted us that afternoon, Isis belongs to me."

That dog, belonging to the owners of a cottage nearby, had prevented their kisses from becoming something more. At the time, he'd thanked the dog to keep him from losing his head. In hindsight, he wished the dog had never found them.

Felicity scooted toward Isis and held out her hand so Isis could sniff her. "Aren't you a pretty girl?" Isis cocked her head, and Felicity stroked her soft, short fur. "Calder, she's lovely." Felicity met his gaze, and he was immediately overcome with a wave of longing—followed by discomfort.

After shunning emotions, particularly pleasant ones, for so long, it was overwhelming to feel so much at once.

"I imagine she must make you happy," Felicity said, continuing to pet Isis as she looked between the greyhound and Calder.

He didn't respond. He never felt *happy*. Isis did, however, make him feel...lighter.

Felicity moved closer to him, her hand resting on the back of Isis's neck. "Calder, why are you like this? What happened? Is this all because of what your father did?"

She was referring to his interference in their relationship, but it was so much more than that. Again, he ignored her. He reached for a slice of cheese and took a bite.

"I wish you would talk to me," she said. "I could help."

He swallowed and fixed her with a frigid stare. "I don't need help. And I don't need to talk to you or anyone else." He ought to toss her out, but damn

if he could bring himself to end the nicest afternoon he'd had in years.

He also realized he wasn't helping it stay nice.
He was such a beast.

She narrowed her eyes at him before turning
her focus to Isis. "I think your master wants me to
leave him alone. I don't really want to because I
would love to find the Calder I knew before. However, I realize that was a long time ago. So perhaps
I should focus on the present." She tipped her head
to the side and looked back to Calder. "I'll stop
bothering you if you agree to allow Bianca to hold
the St. Stephen's Day party here."

"That's extortion."

"Not really. You are in complete control of the
situation. You can throw me out at any moment
and never speak to me again. I'm merely trying to
use any method of persuasion I can. I'll continue to
harangue you about your ghastly behavior unless
you agree to my terms."

"And how will you do that if I throw you out
and never speak to you again?"

She was quiet a moment, then her eyes lit with
inspiration. "I'll make signs and post them outside
your house and in Hartwell. Their purpose will be
to make you laugh—or at least smile."

He nearly did both right then. He had to credit
her ingenuity. "So you really aren't going to stop
bothering me, despite the deal you offered?"

"I suppose not. However, if you allow the party
to be held here, I won't make any signs. Not yet. I
do still have other demands, but we can discuss
those another time."

"What demands are those?" Why was he asking?
It was as if he might consider them.

"Fixing Hartwell House—it's in dire need of repair, and the new Shield's End won't be ready for

quite some time. Besides, Hartwell House is to be used as a school, so it must be refurbished."

"Hartwell House is not my responsibility, whatever it's to be used for."

"I would argue it is—you're the leader of this community. Or you should be. And leaders should use their resources to help those less fortunate." She—and Isis—stared at him.

Calder felt rather defensive in the face of both of them. He didn't appreciate his dog siding with the woman who'd broken his heart. Except had she, if his father had orchestrated the entire scheme?

No, but it was far easier for him to continue believing it was her fault. If he didn't...

"You're correct in that I'm the leader in this community. Hartwell House should be a workhouse, not a free boardinghouse as it is now. I plan to change that."

Felicity looked at him with affront. "You can't dictate what Mrs. Armstrong does with her property."

Calder ignored her outrage. "You said demands, plural. What's the other one?"

She took a deep breath, her eyes narrowing briefly before she answered, "Giving Bianca her settlement."

How dare she meddle in his family's affairs? He stood and gestured for Isis to come to his side. The greyhound obeyed and moved to stand next to him. "Now I *am* throwing you out."

Felicity pursed her lips. "That's what did it?"

"My family is none of your concern. That you would seek to stick your nose into such matters speaks ill of your breeding."

She snorted, then got to her feet. Calder

stepped forward and clasped her arm to provide aid.

Her gaze snapped to his, and a spell fell over him. The picnic from the past was real, the heat of the day, the dazzling joy of her presence.

"That sounds like something your father would have said." Her words jarred him back to the present. Yes, he would have—and often had—commented on her lack of breeding. It was why he hadn't deemed her an appropriate wife.

Was she trying to say he was his father?

It was perhaps the most offensive thing she could say to him. "My father would have given Bianca that money as well as his approval for her marriage simply because Buckleigh became the earl. If he hadn't inherited, my father would have done the same as I did. *My* refusal to give approval is because of who I know Buckleigh to be—a brutal fighter with an inability to control himself. So do not compare me to a man who only cared about a person's position and not their character."

His voice had risen as he'd spoken. He'd actually felt...impassioned. His heart had picked up speed, and a tremor of satisfaction tripped through him.

"I see," she murmured. "I didn't realize those things about Ash. I believe he has a condition that is sometimes difficult for him to manage. I know for certain he isn't brutal and that he adores your sister. He would do anything for her."

Calder didn't wish to hear any of that. He knew his sister was happy, and he didn't care. "It's past time for you to go."

"Yes, I daresay it is," she said on a sigh. "We're settled on the St. Stephen's Day party, then. You'll let Bianca have it here. Thank you, Calder."

He wanted to dispute her, but the words

wouldn't form. She continued, "I will return to discuss these other matters after you've had time to think upon them, particularly your sister. If you don't reconcile with her and make things right, you'll regret it. Don't allow a mistake to fester. I wish to God I'd gone to see you ten years ago—after I received that forged letter. Then maybe things would have been different."

Calder couldn't breathe. It was as if a pile of rocks had fallen on top of him and was pressing him into the ground. And the ground would swallow him whole, just as it had done to Felicity in his nightmare.

"Please go." The words came out low and hard. When her gaze dipped to the picnic, he realized all of it belonged to her.

He turned on his heel and stalked from the room, Isis trotting beside him.

"I'll see you soon," Felicity called after him.

Calder wanted to feel dread, but instead, there was anticipation. And that scared him more than anything ever could.

CHAPTER 5

*A*s Felicity's coach bore her back to Hartwell, she couldn't stop thinking of Calder. He'd actually *laughed*. Until he'd tried to cover it with a cough. But she'd caught it, and she was fairly certain he knew she'd caught it. His guard had been firmly in place after that.

The man she'd loved was in there somewhere. She knew it with a deep certainty that filled her with hope—and despair. He kept himself so buried, so cut off from everyone, that she feared he didn't know how to do anything else.

His defense of his actions regarding Bianca had perhaps been the most telling. He'd created a narrative in which he was the opposite of his father and nothing else mattered. At least that was what Felicity suspected. The man had a grip on his son, even in death, and Felicity hoped she could break it. For Calder's sake. Even if they had no future together, and she honestly wasn't sure they did, he deserved to be happy.

Right now, he was decidedly *not*.

She wasn't going to give up, however. Not when she was seeing cracks in his façade. She could also see how much he cared for his sister, even if he'd behaved like a terrible miser.

Thinking of Bianca, Felicity wanted to tell her what Calder had said, but wasn't sure she should. She'd bristled at being thought of as meddling— she preferred to think of it as helping.

She would, however, write to Bianca immediately and tell her the St. Stephen's Day party would be at Hartwood. If Felicity accomplished nothing else, she'd at least done that.

As the coach neared her cottage, Felicity saw another vehicle parked in front. Her coach stopped, and the coachman helped her out before taking the equipage to the stable down the street.

Felicity didn't recognize the coach, but there was a crest emblazoned on the door. She also didn't recognize that, but the presence of a stag gave her an inkling.

She went inside, where Agatha met her, taking Felicity's cloak, hat, and gloves. "Good afternoon, Mrs. Garland. You've two visitors who asked to wait for you. They are in the parlor. Your mother is resting, and I didn't wish to disturb her."

"Thank you." Felicity had given the maid of all work explicit instructions that Mama needed rest in order to fully recuperate. She turned and went to the parlor and was unsurprised to find Bianca and Poppy seated on the settee. "Good afternoon," she greeted them.

Bianca gave her a sheepish smile. "I hope you don't mind us waiting here for you. It's just… I knew you were visiting Calder today, and I'm afraid I was too excited to wait for word about what happened."

"Bianca's excitement can be difficult to contain," Poppy added with a grin. "I should also admit I was eager to hear the results of your meeting.

When Bianca told me you'd actually persuaded Calder to reconsider, I was flabbergasted."

Felicity sat in a chair near the fireplace to warm herself after the ride from Hartwood. "What will your reaction be when I tell you that you may host the party at Hartwood?"

Poppy and Bianca exchanged looks, their mouths dropping open. Then they both laughed with glee.

"Tell us how you managed it!" Bianca said, leaning forward.

"A slight bit of extortion, I suppose. I threatened to continue harassing him if he didn't change his mind."

"And that worked?"

"I might have suggested putting up signs to pester him. In the end, I simply gave him no opportunity to refuse."

Bianca crowed, and Poppy giggled. "Splendid," Poppy said, then sobered. "But I hate that it's come to that."

"I will employ whatever measures are necessary," Felicity said. "I've warned him I am not finished, that we still need to discuss Hartwell House and Bianca's settlement."

Poppy's eyes widened. "You talked to him about Bianca?" She shook her head. "I can't imagine he took that very well."

"He did not, but he wasn't rude either. He actually had a—somewhat—reasonable explanation for doing what he did."

Bianca gaped at her. "He was reasonable?"

"He said he couldn't approve your marriage because he didn't think Ash would be a good husband."

"Because of his fighting and his affliction." Bianca scoffed. "He said the same to me, and I told him it was nonsense. Ash is the best of men. Certainly a better husband than Calder would be."

Inwardly, Felicity winced. She'd once dreamed of Calder being her husband. But she couldn't dispute what Bianca said. "I didn't say I agreed with him. I told him Ash adored you."

"He does," Poppy agreed, sliding a warm smile toward her sister. "And that should be enough."

"I think he could come around," Felicity said cautiously. "I saw a hint of the young man I knew. He's in there still."

Both sisters stared at her as if she'd gone mad. "Truly?" Poppy whispered, sounding hopeful.

"How can you tell?" Bianca sounded dubious.

"He laughed."

The looks Bianca and Poppy exchanged next were beyond incredulous. Poppy spoke first. "Are you sure?"

Felicity nodded. "I mean to continue my assault."

"To what end?" Bianca asked. "Is your goal just to have Hartwell House repaired?"

"And your settlement delivered," Felicity said.

Bianca eyed her with suspicion. "You have no other motive?"

"I think Bianca is trying to ascertain whether there could be a future for you and our brother," Poppy said drily. "We would dearly love to see him happy, and we wonder if you could bring that about."

Felicity clasped her hands together in her lap. "I think Calder will have to be the one to bring it about. But I should like to help him in any way I can."

"Blast it all, I am going to be blunt," Bianca rushed to say. "Is there any chance you might want to marry Calder? You did once, right?"

"I did, yes." Felicity wouldn't—and *couldn't*—commit to anything else. "I don't know what the future holds for me or for him. I will remind you that I don't live here. I live in York."

"Oh." Bianca settled back on the settee, looking disappointed. "I didn't realize."

"I only came to help my mother. However, I am rather excited about the changes coming with Hartwell House and Shield's End. I may decide to stay, at least for a while."

"I hope you will," Poppy said. "Especially if you're successful in persuading Calder to repair Hartwell House. You will be personally invested in how it all works out."

Yes, she would be. In fact, she wanted to be invested financially too. "I have a bit of money from my husband, and I'd like to give what I can to support the restoration of Hartwell House. Who is managing that fund?"

"Gabriel," Poppy answered, referring to her husband. "I'll tell him you'd like to help. Thank you so much. You should visit Hartwell House."

"I should. It's been years—my father used to take vegetables to Mr. and Mrs. Armstrong."

"Mrs. Armstrong would be delighted to see you," Poppy said before glancing over at her sister. "And she's going to be thrilled to hear about St. Stephen's Day. She was not looking forward to transporting all the children to Thornhill."

Bianca's eyes shone with gratitude. "We can't thank you enough for making this happen. I'll send word to Thornhill straightaway so we can have all the supplies sent to Hartwood." She cocked her head. "Calder still doesn't want anything to do with the event?"

"He hasn't said." But Felicity would ask—he should attend, not just because these were his people, but because he would enjoy it. If he could allow himself to.

"I think we should spend Christmas there," Bianca declared. "That way, we can oversee everything. It's too far to come on the morning of the twenty-sixth, and what if the weather doesn't cooperate?"

"That's been my greatest concern about going to Thornhill," Poppy said. "If it rains too much or snows, no one would be able to attend." She gave her sister a worried look. "Will Calder mind having us there? It would be so lovely to spend Christmas together as a family."

Bianca nodded in agreement. "But only if he accepts Ash and isn't ill-tempered."

"I would love to share my news with him." Poppy's hand drifted across her belly, and Felicity understood immediately what she meant. "I don't know if he'd tell me he was happy for us, but I'd like to think he would."

"You're expecting a child?" Felicity asked. At Poppy's nod, she continued, "My most heartfelt congratulations to you and your husband. You must be thrilled."

"More than I could ever say. After nearly three years of marriage, I'd given up." Pink dotted her cheeks, and her eyes widened briefly. "My apologies. I don't mean to be insensitive."

"You aren't," Felicity said with genuine warmth. "I was married to James for seven years, and we were never blessed with a child." Felicity had become pregnant twice, but hadn't managed to carry the babe long enough. Then, in the latter years of their marriage, James hadn't been able to...perform. She'd accepted the fact that she would be childless. Unless she married again. "I'm so happy for you and your husband."

"Thank you," Poppy said. "It's still very early, but I am surprisingly unconcerned. I just know this child is meant to be, that he—or she—came at precisely the right moment."

Felicity wanted to believe that things happened for a reason. How else could she manage to live with what Calder's father had done? She had to cling to the fact that she was meant to marry James, that the happy times they'd shared were necessary to her life. But what was the reason for Calder? What had happened to him in the last decade that could possibly have been necessary to his life?

Maybe that was a good explanation for what had happened to Calder. He couldn't find meaning in any of it, so he was just...lost.

Well, Felicity had found him. And she wasn't going to let him go.

~

*W*ith Christmas in just five days, an aura of festive jubilance permeated Hartwell. Calder strode along the main street as the shadows grew and the temperature dropped in the late afternoon. It would be close to freezing in a couple of hours, if not below that.

A shiver danced over Calder's shoulders, and he burrowed deeper into his greatcoat. Up ahead, the Silver Goat, Hartwell's coaching inn, beckoned with a warm hearth and lively company.

Not that Calder wanted the latter, nor would anyone seek to have him there. Everyone he passed eyed him with awe and maybe an edge of fear. What else should he expect after removing himself completely from this community? Not to mention everything he'd done to project the notion that he didn't want to be a part of it. He'd refused to host their annual holiday party. He didn't support Hartwell House. He did nothing to endear himself to anyone.

And he'd been fine with that—until Felicity.

She had him second-guessing everything. He'd spent the last two days since her surprise picnic in a foul mood.

Scowling, he strode past the inn, pausing to look in the wide front window. A group of people were gathered around a table laughing. Behind them, near the wall, a couple met beneath the mistletoe. They glanced around to see if anyone watched them, and when it seemed they didn't, their lips met for a sweet, lingering kiss.

An image of him kissing Felicity beneath the mistletoe sprang to his mind. A fierce wave of longing washed over him.

He scowled again and moved on, turning down a side street. A handful of children played up ahead, their shouts and giggles providing a beautiful accompaniment to the charming winter scene.

Calder abruptly turned down a narrow lane and emerged on the next street. He steered to the right and watched as a woman helped an older man into a cottage. The door closed, but Calder watched them through the window as she helped settle him into a chair near the fire. She wrapped a blanket around him, and a younger girl came in to hug him. She sat on a footstool and spoke to him animatedly while the man, her grandfather maybe, laughed.

The woman returned with a tray of refreshments and set it on a table, then began to pour tea. The girl snatched a biscuit from the tray and went to the corner. Music from a pianoforte filled the air. Calder leaned against a tree and listened, the bitter cold of the late afternoon forgotten.

After a few minutes, another man came into the room. He swept the woman into his arms and kissed her cheek before whispering something in her ear. She laughed, and they parted, bowing to each other before launching into a makeshift reel.

The music continued, and the old man grinned as he watched them. Round and round they danced. Calder stood there, utterly enchanted. He'd never seen anything so beautiful. An ache formed in his chest and spread through him. He wanted that. Desperately.

The pianoforte—rather the gifted musician plucking its keys—built to a crescendo, and the dance came to an end. Everyone inside broke into mad applause, and Calder found himself doing the same.

The old man's gaze seemed to find him, piercing Calder with a bright intensity. He lifted his teacup in a silent toast before returning his attention to his family.

Family.

That was what Calder wanted. That was what he was missing.

Darkness swept through him, and he pushed away from the tree, blindly stumbling along until he realized where he was. Felicity's cottage—rather, her mother's—stood across the lane.

Before he could think better of his actions, he strode to the front door and knocked. A moment later, the door opened to reveal Felicity.

Her green eyes widened in surprise. "Calder?" She looked past him. "Is everything all right?"

No. "May I come in?"

"Of course." She opened the door wider and

ushered him inside. "Let me take your hat and your coat."

He doffed the garments, handing them to her so she could hang them on a rack by the door. He removed his gloves and shoved them into the pockets of his greatcoat and almost immediately regretted the actions. Why had he come here? He couldn't stay.

She seemed to read his mind, for she took his hand and drew him into the front parlor, a small, cozy room with a blazing fire and bedecked with greenery. He looked about for mistletoe and was disappointed to find there wasn't any. And why should there be? It was her mother's house, and her mother was a widow.

As was Felicity.

He'd never been more aware of that fact. Perhaps because her hand was still clasping his. The feel of her bare flesh against him made the longing he'd felt a little while ago fade into nothingness. He wanted to pull her to him and kiss her, mistletoe or not.

Instead, he let go of her hand and moved to the hearth to warm himself, if that was possible. Sometimes he feared he was frigid at his very core. The name Chill fit him to perfection—or was it that he'd made himself align with the name?

"I'm delighted to see you," she said. "Would you like tea? Or perhaps sherry? I'm afraid I don't have any brandy."

"Nothing, thank you." *Just you.*

She nodded, then clasped her hands briefly in front of her before dropping them to her sides. Was she nervous? Good. He was too.

"What brings you here?" She stepped toward him, and he turned so they could face each other in front of the fire.

"I was just walking through the village and found myself here."

"So you didn't come to speak with me? About Hartwell House or anything else?"

He made a faint sound low in his throat. "I don't want to talk about that. Or St. Stephen's Day." Both his sisters had sent notes thanking him for changing his mind, even though he didn't recall actually doing that. Felicity had managed him rather well.

Poppy and Bianca had also asked if they might celebrate Christmas at Hartwood with him. The thought of them doing so had made him crumple both letters and throw them into the fire.

Family.

He had one, and if he could just... What? He had to do *something*, but he didn't know what. Did he think Felicity could help him? Yes, because she'd reawakened everything he'd buried. Everything he'd thought was dead.

"What do you want to talk about, then?" she asked softly, almost shyly. He was assaulted by the memory of her at eighteen. She'd been shocked when the Earl of Chilton had danced with her at the summer assembly. That had been the single greatest dance of his life.

He suddenly wished they had a pianoforte and someone to play it.

He returned his mind to her question. "I don't know. I just wanted to come inside." To see her. To feel her. "All I do since you returned is feel things. I don't like feeling things."

"Why not?"

"It's easier not to. My father didn't like it when I felt things. He said dukes needed to be above all that."

"Your father isn't here anymore, and even if he

was, it doesn't matter what he wanted or what he told you to be. You get to be who you want." She edged closer and lightly placed her hand on his chest, her palm pressing against his lapel. "Who do you want to be, Calder?"

Her touch was sun to the dark landscape of his soul. "I don't know." If she was touching him, perhaps that meant he could touch her. He reached for her face, cupping her gently, then stroking his thumb down her cheek and along her jaw.

Her eyes narrowed seductively, and his body jerked to full sensual awareness. His cock thickened, and he yearned to take her in his arms.

He frowned, glancing up toward the ceiling. "Why don't you have any mistletoe?"

She laughed softly, and it was the music he was missing. "Because I'm a fool. I never imagined I'd need it." She slid her hand up his coat and circled it around his neck. Her fingertips slipped into the hair at his nape. "I was wrong."

"I should say so," he murmured before he lowered his mouth to hers.

This was madness. *This* was wrong. He had no business kissing her, and yet he couldn't have stopped himself if the ocean had washed over him and swept him from the shore.

It was as if no time had passed but also forever. He wrapped his arms around her and held her tight to his chest. She clutched at his neck while molding her mouth to his. Then she opened, meeting his tongue and ravishing him as surely as he wanted to ravish her.

Groaning softly, he plundered her mouth, telling her in the only way he knew how that he wanted her. Needed her. That she was the very thing his dark heart needed to heal—if it ever could.

Their embrace was thunder and bliss, a joining ten years in the making, a dream he'd never thought would come true. She hadn't abandoned him. She'd been taken from him, and he from her. This was the future they'd promised each other. Or at least, it could be.

Unless he messed it up.

He pulled back, taking his mouth from hers and setting her back to the floor—he'd completely swept her up against him. They breathed heavily as they stared at each other, still so close.

"You're in there," she whispered. "The man I loved."

Loved. Past tense. He loved her in the present and would always love her. But what was love when it came from someone who caused misery?

He took another step back. "I'll consider Hartwell House."

"You should visit," she said softly. Her pulse beat strongly in her throat, just beneath the sweep of her jaw, and her rapid breaths caused her chest to rise and fall in quick succession. She was a woman enraptured. He tried not to stare.

"I'll think about it." He pivoted, his feet like lead. He should go, but couldn't bring himself to.

"Please stop in anytime." She touched him again, her hand on his bicep. The connection galvanized him.

He stalked toward the door. "Thank you." He didn't turn to look at her before going into the entry hall, where he slammed his hat on his head and swept his coat into his arms. He waited to don the garment until he was outside where it was full dusk. The icy cold of oncoming night crashed into him, banishing the heat that had sparked between him and Felicity.

Not banishing it, no. Abating it. He now wondered if he would forever burn for her, if he always had and just hadn't known it.

He buttoned his coat and pulled on his gloves as he reached the street. Turning his head, he saw her standing in the doorway watching him. She was going to catch a chill—and not just from the near-freezing temperature.

He was Chill, or had been all his life until he'd become the duke. The name now seemed prophetic, considering how he'd turned out. She was warmth and light and cheer, everything he was not. For that reason, he should stay far, far away from her.

CHAPTER 6

*B*uilt in the early seventeenth century, Hartwell House was a gorgeous manor home with cream-colored stone and five stately gables. Looking at the structure, one could not discern its disrepair. It exuded charm and warmth, which made sense because it was a home to so many in need of one.

Felicity exited her coach and hurried to the front door. The weather had remained icy cold today. In fact, there had been ice hanging from the cottage that morning. For this reason, Felicity had begged her mother to stay home where it was warm, and she wouldn't risk catching a chill. Mama had been happy to oblige despite wanting to visit Hartwell House.

The door opened before Felicity could knock. Mrs. Armstrong stood inside the threshold, grinning widely. A woman in her late forties with mostly dark hair—there was gray at her temples—she was the overseer of the Institution for Impoverished Women. "My goodness, it's Felicity Templeton! Come in, come in." She ushered Felicity into the hall and quickly divested her of her cloak, hat, and muff.

Felicity pulled her gloves off, smiling. "I'm Mrs. Garland now."

"Of course you are, but to me, you shall always be Felicity Templeton—that's who you were last time I saw you!" She winked at Felicity, then took her gloves. "I'll make sure these are warmed up so they'll be nice and toasty when you go. And I'll fetch some tea. I'm sure that won't come amiss."

"It will not, thank you," Felicity said.

Mrs. Armstrong gestured toward a sitting room just off the entry hall. "There's a nice fire in there."

Felicity left the entry hall with its dark wood paneling and moved into the sitting room. She gravitated toward the fire to warm herself. Despite the warming pan in her coach and the relatively short drive to Hartwell House, she was rather chilled.

A movement to the right caught her eye. She saw a small boot disappear beneath a long settee. Smiling, she held her hands to the fire. "Are you playing hide and seek?" she asked.

"No, but that sounds fun. Can we?"

Felicity laughed, then turned so that her backside was to the fire. A young boy of maybe seven slithered out from beneath the settee. He glanced toward the doorway. "I'm not supposed to be here."

"Oh. Well, then perhaps you should go."

He nodded. "I just wanted to see the carving on the mantel. I'm trying to draw it." He held up a piece of parchment filled with illustrations.

Felicity gave him a questioning look. "May I?"

He handed her the paper, and she gently took it between her hands to more closely see the drawings. "Did you draw these?"

He nodded.

"You are exceptionally skilled. I love this bird." Her gaze caught on a small falcon perched on a fence post. He'd captured the animal's intelligent eyes and the delicate lines of each feather.

She glanced toward the mantel and saw that it was intricately carved with leaves and flowers. She searched the paper and finally found his rendering of some of the flora, but it was very small. "I think you need another piece of paper."

"Parchment is hard to come by," he said matter-of-factly. "I use every last inch. That's what Mrs. Armstrong says to do." He looked toward the door again. "If she catches me here outside of our appointed time, I won't be allowed to visit for a week."

That seemed a trifle harsh, but Felicity had no idea what it took to manage an institution like this with all the women and their children. She imagined it was a challenge to maintain some semblance of order.

"Then, I suppose you better go." She handed the paper back to him. "Could you use more parchment, then?"

He grinned, revealing a gap between his front teeth, which seemed to just be coming in. "Always!" Then he disappeared from the room in a flash.

Mrs. Armstrong returned a moment later with a tea tray, which she set on a table near the hearth. "Do you take any milk or sugar?"

"A bit of both, thank you." Felicity perched on the settee the boy had hidden beneath. "I was sorry to hear about Mr. Armstrong."

Mrs. Armstrong handed Felicity her cup. "Thank you, dear. But then you're a widow now too—and so young. Have you any children?" She fixed herself a cup of tea and then sat on the settee opposite Felicity.

"No, we didn't have any children." Felicity drank her tea, welcoming the warmth of the brew.

"We didn't either, which is how Hartwell House came to be. We took in a young woman and her baby. Then another." Mrs. Armstrong sipped her tea.

Felicity hadn't realized the Armstrongs didn't have children of their own, but then she'd been rather young when she'd left Hartwell. "It's a wonderful institution, such a necessary alternative to a workhouse, where mothers are separated from their children."

"Yes, though our secret is out, I'm afraid. We've had more women arriving so far this fall and winter than ever before. I tried turning people away for lack of room, but they beg to sleep on the floor if we've nothing else. I don't have the heart to turn them out into the cold. Lord Darlington has temporarily housed a few people in cottages at his estate, which has been a help."

Felicity was more determined than ever to help. "I understand Hartwell House is in need of repairs. I was hoping you might give me a tour? I'd like to donate some money to your cause and see about getting more." Aside from convincing Calder to do his part, she thought of people she could ask in York to contribute.

"You're very kind," Mrs. Armstrong said. "I'd be delighted to give you a tour, and truly, if you have the inclination to come and spend time with the children—reading stories to them or even teaching them skills—we'd all be grateful."

Felicity thought of the boy she'd met and wondered if he could teach her how to draw. "I would be honored to spend time here."

Mrs. Armstrong smiled before drinking more of her tea. She stood and set the cup on the tray. "Shall we take the tour?"

"Yes." Felicity finished her tea and placed her cup next to Mrs. Armstrong's.

Over the next half hour, Mrs. Armstrong showed her the entirety of Hartwell House, from the uppermost rooms, where a few maids—all women who'd come here in search of shelter and care at some point—resided to the dormitory that housed other women to individual rooms shared by mothers with their children. There was also a schoolroom, an exercise room where the smaller children could run and play when the weather was poor, and a large dining room. Some of the bedrooms leaked, and they were in need of more furniture, namely beds. There was much that could be done, and she was angry with Calder for not continuing his father's support.

At the conclusion of the tour, they neared the small room near the kitchen that Mrs. Armstrong indicated she used as an office. "Is there anything I can readily obtain for you in the near term? Or for the children, especially with Christmas nearly upon us?" Felicity already planned to gather all the parchment she could find in Hartwell.

"We had a lovely St. Nicholas Day party here. The residents received gifts from Lord and Lady Darlington as well as Lord and Lady Buckleigh."

Felicity wished she'd known of it, for she would have come too. She was not surprised when Mrs. Armstrong didn't mention Calder's name. "That sounds as if it was a wonderful event."

Mrs. Armstrong nodded. "Everyone is looking forward to St. Stephen's Day. I'm so relieved it will be at Hartwood. I wasn't relishing having to transport the children to Thornhill. In fact, I'd begun to consider just doing my best to host something here."

Felicity was now doubly pleased she'd arranged

for the party to be held at Hartwood. "I'm glad you don't have to."

A figure emerged from the kitchen and stopped short upon seeing them. Poppy grinned. "Felicity, how lovely to see you here."

"Mrs. Armstrong was just showing me all the wonderful things she's done."

"Oh, stop," Mrs. Armstrong said, blushing. "I'm going to my office now before either of you can embarrass me." She flashed them both a grateful smile, then ducked into her office.

"Are you staying long?" Poppy asked.

"No, I was just about to go, in fact."

"I'll walk out with you." Poppy stuck her head into Mrs. Armstrong's office to say she was leaving. Felicity did the same, and they exchanged farewells before Poppy and Felicity started toward the entry hall.

"Felicity, I must thank you again for whatever influence you have with Calder."

Felicity wasn't sure what Poppy could be thinking of. Yesterday he'd refused to talk about anything—he'd been upset. And then he'd kissed her, and everything had gone absolutely sideways. He *had* said he'd think about helping here at Hartwell House...

"Did he reinstate the dukedom's support of Hartwell House?" Felicity asked.

"Not that I'm aware. Did you persuade him to do that too?"

"I didn't think so. What are you talking about, then?"

"He's invited us to spend Christmas at Hartwood." She cocked her head from one side to the other. "Perhaps the word 'invited' is a tad excessive. He wrote and said that if we wanted to come to Hartwood on Christmas Eve so that we could be there to help prepare for St. Stephen's Day, he would appreciate it. Because he doesn't want anything to do with it." She rolled her eyes. "Still the same icy Calder, but it's a move in the right direction at least."

While Felicity was angry with him for turning his back on Hartwell House, she also understood he was a man burdened with pain and loneliness brought on by horrible expectations. She'd begun to suspect that his father's actions toward him ran deeper than verbal cruelty, but she was terrified to learn the truth. "I'm so glad you and Bianca haven't given up on him."

"We never will," she said quietly but fiercely. "And I'm so grateful you haven't either. I know your presence has made an impression."

"I didn't say anything to him about having you for Christmas." Felicity wanted Poppy to give Calder credit, not her.

"Well, I still think you played a part, whether you did so on purpose or not." She took Felicity's hand and gave it a quick, heartfelt squeeze. "Honestly, I'll take any positivity from him any way I can." She smiled before reaching for her cloak.

Felicity was as surprised by Calder's Christmas invitation as Poppy appeared to be. He was so vulnerable, so fragile... The things he'd said to her yesterday about not wanting to feel tore at her heart. He needed care and understanding—and she knew his sisters would give it to him if he allowed them the chance. It seemed he might be ready, or almost ready, to do that.

"You should come too," Poppy said as she pulled on her hat.

Felicity donned her cloak. "I couldn't. I haven't been invited." And she felt strongly he had to invite her. Having his sisters there was likely going to be challenging enough. If he was going to try feeling emotions again, it was probably best if he didn't try to manage too much at once.

Poppy nodded. "I understand. Bianca and I are foolishly hoping you and he will find your way back to one another."

So was Felicity. She sent Poppy an earnest look. "Give him time and don't let go. He needs you, but he'll never say so."

Poppy nodded, and Felicity thought she saw moisture in her gray-blue eyes.

"I nearly forgot!" Mrs. Armstrong's voice rang in the hall, disrupting the taut moment. "Both of your gloves are nice and warm." She handed a pair of gloves to both Felicity and Poppy.

As Felicity drew hers on, she sighed with pleasure. "Oh, these are lovely. Thank you."

Poppy leaned toward her and stage-whispered, "This is my favorite part of coming here in the wintertime."

They all laughed, then went their separate ways. As Felicity's coachman opened the door to her carriage, she asked him to make a slight detour on their way home.

A short while later, they crested a small rise, and her childhood home came into view. She'd managed to be here the last several weeks without seeing it. Why? Because it reminded her of her father and of her lost innocence. Of Calder and the way he'd broken her heart.

Only he hadn't. They'd been victims of his father's machinations. And her father's, somewhat. She had forgiven Papa, but his actions still stung. She wished he were still alive so she could talk to him about it. Maybe that would make what he'd done easier to understand.

Or not. She wasn't sure there was any way to defend his behavior.

The two-story farmhouse looked the same, with its cheery mullioned windows and charming fence with the gate her father had built with the letter T leading up the walkway to the front door.

Her breath caught when the door opened and out bounded a familiar dog.

Isis leapt into the yard and dashed about for a minute before going to relieve herself. Calder came out onto the stoop and looked about, his gaze settling on Isis as she finished her business.

Felicity knocked on the roof of the coach, and the driver knew to pull to the house and stop—she'd told him she might want to. She'd had no idea if anyone lived there. And now it seemed…Calder did?

Not just because he'd come outside with his dog, but because smoke curled from the chimney, indicating it wasn't a quick visit to check on the property. Or maybe it was, and he just preferred to linger. Her heart twisted—he was so incredibly complicated.

Felicity watched out the window as the coach pulled up in front of the house. Calder stepped from the stoop and moved along the path until he reached the gate.

The coachman helped her out, and she told him she'd just be a few minutes. Calder opened the gate for her as she approached, and they walked along the path in silence for a moment. Isis chased a bird who'd had the nerve to land on a fence post.

"What are you doing here?" Felicity asked.

He looked at her askance, a hint of amusement —amusement!—hovering over his mouth. "I could ask you the same."

"I haven't come by since I returned to Hartwell. I was curious. I never imagined to find you here."

"The estate owns it. I didn't know that until I inherited and read through all my father's account books. There was a great deal he didn't tell me." If that was meant to be a veiled comment about the horrible secret the former duke had kept from all of them, she was impressed with how little vitriol Calder's tone carried.

He opened the door to the house. "Do you want to go inside?"

"Please."

He gestured for her to precede him. She walked into the hall, which was flanked by two rooms, one her mother had used for their formal receiving room and the other they'd used as a library and family parlor. She went into the latter and saw that the furniture was the same.

"It looks exactly as I remember," she said softly as she moved about the room, trailing her gloved fingers over a table, the back of a settee, and the mantel. A warm fire heated her as she turned and took in the familiar space. "Why is it the same?"

He stood in the doorway to the hall, Isis at his side, looking distinctly uncomfortable. "I suppose whoever lived here after you left kept everything."

"Where are they now?"

He shrugged. "The house was empty when I inherited." He moved into the room, keeping his gaze from meeting hers. "I like to spend time here when I want to be alone."

Except as far as she could tell, he was *always* alone. Which meant he came here for another reason, at least partially. She wouldn't press him. "I just came from Hartwell House. I have a list of repairs—rather, I can draft one for you. The house requires general maintenance as well as more furniture." She looked around the room. "We could start with what's here."

His eyes met hers with a look of astonishment. "You'd give your family's things away?"

"They're not doing anyone any good here," she said. "At Hartwell House, they will be put to good use."

Calder stood near the window, through which Felicity could see her coach. She couldn't leave the coachman waiting long, not in this cold.

"Calder, I somewhat understand why you stopped giving money to Hartwell House, but you must see that they need it. Surely you can spare enough to see the building repaired at the very least. They are in dire need."

"You 'somewhat understand'? How is that?" His tone held a dark, mocking edge.

"I comprehend that you don't wish to do anything your father did. Since he supported Hartwell House, you will not."

"Or perhaps I'm just a coldhearted monster who doesn't want to help others."

She snorted. "I don't believe that any more than you do." She was fibbing a bit—she wasn't sure if he believed that about himself or not. "I see a man who loves his dog and his sisters." She walked toward him, slowly, as if she could frighten him if she moved too quickly.

He didn't budge as she approached. "Will you ever stop pestering me?"

"No. At least not until you're yourself again. I'll be right here for however long that takes." She stopped directly in front of him so that they nearly touched.

"Felicity, I am not the dream you remember. I am cruel and horrible, exactly the way I was raised to be. As it happens, I *will* repair Hartwell House so that I can then turn it into a workhouse."

She knew he didn't mean it. He was trying to push her away because she'd said she would stay as long as it took. "Mrs. Armstrong will never allow that."

"She will if I offer her a large sum of money. People will do anything for blunt."

The truth hit her hard and fast, particularly standing here in this room—her home—a place her father had forsaken for nothing more than money. "Please don't do that," she pleaded. "You don't have to do that to drive me away. I'll leave if you ask me to."

His jaw worked, and he opened his mouth. But nothing came out before he snapped it closed.

"Do you want me to go?" she asked.

He looked utterly conflicted, his eyes blazing as if a war were being fought just behind them.

Felicity realized she'd pushed him far enough today. He was making progress—with his sister, and with Hartwell House. Perhaps she could make one more attempt...

She lifted her hands to his shoulders. "Just visit Hartwell House and see for yourself. I agree that you *will* repair it, and the idea of a workhouse will be lost completely."

She stood on her toes and pressed her lips to his. She kissed him once, twice, a third time, her mouth lingering beneath his. "And I'm not leaving Hartwell—or you."

Letting him go was difficult. She wanted to enfold him in her arms and show him how much she cared for him, what it would be like if he let himself truly feel.

But she didn't. She stepped back, gave him a

final look that conveyed all the warmth and hope she had for him, then left the house.

She'd come back another day and see the whole thing. Today hadn't been about that or her. It was about Calder and bringing him back. He was so close, and she wasn't giving up until he found peace.

CHAPTER 7

*C*alder's brain hurt. He'd thought and reflected and bloody *felt* more in the past week than he had in the past decade. And what good had it done?

He was allowing the St. Stephen's Day party to happen at Hartwell, something that would have made his father happy, which made Calder decidedly surly.

Then he'd invited his sisters and their husbands to spend Christmas at Hartwood, something else that would have pleased their father. He'd adored them, particularly Bianca, who was the "very image" of their mother, as their father had said a thousand times. And the hell of it was that they adored him. It was a wedge between him and his sisters, invisible to them and insurmountable to him. He could easily tell them why he despised the man they loved, but why ruin their memory of him?

He could hear Felicity now—*See, you are every bit the man I knew you were.*

Maybe. Somewhere deep inside. Somewhere he wanted to keep private and unseen.

And now, here he was at Hartwell House to investigate their needs. All because of Felicity.

The afternoon was slightly warmer than the day before, but still cold enough that he'd brought his coach. He stepped out of the vehicle, and Isis leapt down beside him.

Calder frowned at the manor house. It looked perfectly fine. He knew he was being foolish, that he likely couldn't see its defects. Plus, Felicity had said they needed furniture. He couldn't decide whether there was a deficit unless he went inside.

He didn't particularly want to.

Postponing the inevitable, he walked around the house, sizing up the exterior as best he could. He noted a broken window and a potential leak judging from the water marks on the stone.

Calder realized Isis was no longer with him. He looked around, then saw the greyhound dash by. She picked up a stick with her mouth and trotted back around the corner to the back of the house.

Following her, Calder saw the reason for Isis's distraction. A girl with bright blonde hair patted the dog's head, then threw the stick again. Hell, she had quite a throw.

"Is that your dog?" she asked as he walked over to her.

"Yes."

The girl's mouth drooped with momentary disappointment. "I was hoping she didn't belong to anyone." She sighed. "She's very beautiful."

"I think so too. Her name is Isis." He glanced back at the house as Isis came back and the girl took the stick once more. "Do you live here?" Calder asked.

The girl nodded. "I'm Alice." She threw the stick again, and Isis ran after it like she was a puppy once more. "I wish I could have a dog. But Mrs.

Armstrong says there isn't room for pets. Except her cat, who everyone says is older than any cat should be."

"How old is that?" Calder asked.

The girl's brow creased. "Oh, *very* old. I should say fifteen maybe."

Calder chuckled. "Is that old for a cat or for people too?"

Isis returned with the stick, and Alice took it. Then she blinked up at Calder. "Only for cats, silly. People-old is like you. You must be at least thirty."

Calder's chuckle bloomed into full laughter. "I am in fact thirty. How old are you?"

"Six." She threw the stick. "And a half."

He knew how important that half year could be at her age. "So you'd like to have a dog, but Mrs. Armstrong won't let you have one. What about your mother, what does she say?"

"She wouldn't mind. She thinks my younger brother might like one too."

"You have a younger brother?"

She nodded as Isis ran to her. "Joseph. He's three."

"What happened to your papa?"

"He died." She said this without emotion but managed not to sound cold like Calder did. For her, it was simply a statement of fact, of the reality that was her life.

"I'm sorry to hear that." And he was sorry their little family had needed to rely on the charity of Mrs. Armstrong. Yet it was a far better alternative than a workhouse.

Blast it all, he *was* a monster. He couldn't turn this place into a workhouse. "Do you like living here?" he asked her gently as she continued to throw the stick for Isis.

"Most of the time. Sometimes Mama cries because we can't live in our own house. I only care that we're together. But I wish our room didn't leak." She made a face. "I hate that dripping noise when it rains. I shall be ever so happy when the new institution is built. It won't have a drip." She smiled at him, and the brilliance of it nearly made him weep.

When Isis returned next, she flopped at Alice's feet and let the stick fall to the ground.

"I think that's her way of saying she's tired," Calder said.

"I should go inside anyway. Mama said I shouldn't stay out long because it's so cold." She walked a few feet away and squatted down.

Calder followed her and watched as she picked up a handful of soldiers and a wagon. One of the wheels fell to the ground as she stood.

"Dammit."

Calder blinked at her, his eyes widening. "I beg your pardon?"

She clutched her toys and looked at him, her features frozen. "John says that all the time. It's a naughty word, isn't it?"

"It's not entirely suitable for six—and-a-half—year-old girls."

"Please don't tell Mama. Or Mrs. Armstrong. I won't get any pudding for dessert."

Calder put his hand on his heart. "I swear your secret is safe with me. Dammit." He winked at her, and she giggled. Oh, that sound… He looked at her and saw the future that should have been his—a bright-eyed, blonde-haired little girl with a love for dogs and a penchant for curse words.

He bent and picked up the wheel, then held out his hand for the wagon. "May I try to fix it for you?"

She nodded, handing him the wagon.

Calder studied the toy and realized there was a piece missing. He surveyed the ground and managed to find it. He slid the wheel back onto the axle, then bent to retrieve the missing piece, which he affixed to the end to keep the wheel on. "Here you are." He handed it back to her.

"Thank you, sir."

He noted that the toy soldiers seemed more suited to a boy. "Would you like to have a doll?"

She shrugged. "I s'pose. But I'd rather have more soldiers. And maybe a gun. I asked for one— and a dog—on St. Nicholas Day, but I got these instead."

Calder couldn't help but laugh again. "You want a gun?"

"Yes, so I can shoot Freddie."

Stifling his laughter, Calder adopted his most serious tone—the fact that she wanted to shoot someone was serious. "Who's Freddie?"

"He pulls my hair and steals my biscuits. I don't like him."

"I don't think I like him either. However, shooting him is rather excessive."

"I wouldn't *kill* him," she said sullenly.

"Well, that's good to know. How about you find revenge in another, more fitting, way?"

Calder's mind worked until he settled on a solution. "You say he steals your biscuits?" At her nod, Calder continued. "Next time, put something in your biscuits that would make him scream."

She stared up at him, rapt. "What would make a boy scream?"

"Maggots." Calder knew this from personal experience. When he'd been around Alice's age, he'd hidden food—he couldn't remember nor could he identify what it was—in his room. Sometime later, he'd stumbled upon it only to see it was crawling with maggots. He'd screamed and then he'd been punished for hiding the food.

"On second thought, perhaps you shouldn't do that," he said. "I don't want you to get in trouble."

She shook her head vigorously. "Oh, I won't. He's the one stealing my biscuits, and if he says anything, Mrs. Armstrong will know he's a thief."

"Perhaps the biscuits should be a gift. That way you have no culpability. I'll bring you some, for Freddie, mind you."

"Oh, would you?" Her voice held a hint of awe that was altogether different from the awe bordering on fear that everyone else treated him with.

"Certainly, plus some for you that are maggot-free."

She grinned widely. "I like you almost as much as your dog."

His heart swelled. "That's the nicest compliment I've ever received."

She rolled her eyes. "It is *not*."

It actually was.

A short while later, after watching Alice go back into the house, Calder left without going inside. He didn't need to see the leaks or the furniture that was needed to decide to support Hartwell House. His interlude with Alice had told him everything he needed to know. That Hartwell House needed his help—and dogs—and that he wasn't entirely broken.

Severely damaged, but for the first time, he had hope that he could be fixed. He smiled, thinking of Alice shooting Freddie. That boy was going to be sorry he ever pulled her hair and stole her biscuits.

When Calder went to the kitchen to discuss his very specific biscuit requirements with the cook, all the retainers in the kitchen and scullery had stopped working and tried not to gape.

"Let me understand, Your Grace," the cook said. "You want a half-dozen biscuits with...maggots?"

"Or some sort of vermin that's available at this time of year," he said, realizing maggots could be hard to find in December unless one visited the privy. And he would never ask anyone to do *that*, not even on his most obnoxious day.

"I know just the thing," one of her assistants said. "Worms are available any time of year. Would that suffice?"

"I should think so. There's a girl at Hartwell House who says one of the boys keeps stealing her biscuits. I should like him to stop, and shooting him—that was her solution—seemed inappropriate. Worms in the biscuits he pilfers should put an end to his thievery."

Everyone in the kitchen stared at him. Then the cook began to laugh. Others joined in. Calder found himself smiling.

After a minute, the cook said, "We'll come up with something. He won't be stealing her biscuits again."

"Thank you," Calder said. "I'll need them tomorrow afternoon, along with some that are free of vermin for the girl."

"Oh, we'll make something special just for her." The cook and her assistant shared a look, and Calder couldn't remember the last time he'd felt so...satisfied.

What he wouldn't give to make the sensation last. Too bad it was already starting to fade.

❧

*T*he weather on the day before Christmas Eve was as cold as the prior two days, with an added bonus: the threat of snow. Felicity looked up at the sky as she arrived at Hartwell House with a stack of parchment.

"I don't think it will snow until later, if at all," her coachman noted as he helped her out of the carriage.

"Well, if it does start, we'll leave at once," she said. "I won't be terribly long anyway."

He nodded, then handed her the stack of parchment that Felicity had accumulated. She'd gathered and purchased as much as she could find. "Thank you. Are you going to the stable to warm up?"

"Aye," he said with a grin. "The other day, I had a mug of fine ale as well."

"I'm glad to hear it," Felicity said, chuckling before she turned to go to the door. She knocked, but no one came. Then she heard…screaming?

Frightened for whoever was making the noise, Felicity opened the door and went inside. She quickly deposited the parchment on the long, wooden bench that ran along the right side of the entry hall and hurried toward the sound. A moment later, she walked into the dining hall, where a boy was spitting on the floor and dancing around intermittently yelping. He had been the one screaming?

She started forward to ask if he was all right, but then noticed that the other children were not alarmed. In fact, they were…amused. Why were they laughing at him? And why did the one girl look as if she'd just won a very important contest?

Then Felicity noticed the most astonishing thing of all: Calder stood in the corner, his arms crossed, his face alight with mirth. Mirth? She blinked, certain she was imagining his expression. But no, she wasn't. He was *amused*.

Instead of disrupting whatever was going on,

she skirted the perimeter of the hall until she reached Calder. "What happened?"

"Freddie's had his comeuppance," he said through a smile.

Felicity regarded the scenario. The boy—Freddie, presumably—had stopped moving. His face was pale as he glared at the girl, who still appeared quite pleased with everything.

"What on earth is going on in here?" Mrs. Armstrong entered, trailed by several women, and Felicity wondered how it had taken them so long to arrive. "We go outside for one minute to take a brisk walk around the house, and this is what happens?" She looked at Freddie and the girl. "What *did* happen?" Her eyes narrowed. "Freddie, did you take someone's biscuits again?"

"In fact, he did," Calder answered mildly. "However, I daresay he won't be doing so again. Isn't that right, Freddie?" He looked at the boy with a placid smile that should have scared the impudence right out of him. And maybe it did. Freddie looked as if he were horrified to have a duke, or maybe just a man, since there weren't any in residence, speaking to him. It occurred to Felicity that they could benefit from some male guidance. Perhaps she could convince—

Goodness, what was she *thinking*? She'd already pushed Calder well past his limits.

Mrs. Armstrong exhaled, and another woman came forward. She looked quite angry, her dark eyes fixed on Freddie. "I told you if you committed any other infractions, you would miss the St. Stephen's Day party."

Freddie blanched, then hung his head.

"Apologize to Alice," a woman, likely his mother, said, arriving at his side.

"I'm sorry," he mumbled, his gaze still pinned to the floor.

His mother tapped her foot. "Look at her when you say so."

Freddie lifted his head and regarded the defiant Alice. "I'm sorry I took your biscuits. I won't ever do it again."

"Good. You know what will happen if you do," she warned.

Another woman, this one fair-haired and almost certainly Alice's mother, came from behind Mrs. Armstrong. "Now, Alice, vengeance is not ladylike."

Alice sent Calder a smirk then nodded at the woman. "Yes, Mama."

"I think it's time everyone returned to their rooms for quiet time," Mrs. Armstrong said.

The children broke apart, many of them talking and laughing as they departed. Alice went to Calder and hugged him.

Felicity stared in shock as he hugged her in return and whispered something in her ear. She grinned and nodded, then skipped back to her mother, who looked at Calder in bemusement.

A glance toward Mrs. Armstrong revealed she was staring at him in the same fashion. It seemed every adult in the room was as baffled by Calder's behavior as Felicity was. And why wouldn't they be? Until…today, apparently, he had not been a supporter of Hartwell House. To see that he'd somehow befriended one of the residents and had perhaps played a role in a revenge scheme was utterly amazing.

Felicity might not have believed it if she hadn't seen it.

Except she would have. She knew the real Calder was in there, the one she loved. And yes, she still loved him after all this time. This was simply the proof of what she'd already known to be true. She was particularly glad that others could see it too.

When the room was empty save for Calder, Felicity, and Mrs. Armstrong, the latter frowned before addressing Calder. "Your Grace, I am pleased to see you here. However, I must ask that you not encourage disruptions among the children."

"I doubt he was doing that," Felicity said, feeling the need to come to his defense. She moved to his side. "I've been telling him about all the things you need, and I believe he stopped by to see for himself."

"Yes," Calder said. "I would be pleased if you would accept my support to repair Hartwell House."

Mrs. Armstrong's jaw dropped, but she quickly clamped it shut. Nodding, she seemed at a total loss for words.

Felicity jumped in to fill the silence. "Could you also provide a list of furnishings you need? I know you are short beds, and as it happens, we could have a few delivered tomorrow, perhaps."

"On Christmas Eve?" Mrs. Armstrong asked.

Right, maybe not on Christmas Eve. Or Christmas Day. Or St. Stephen's Day. Goodness, this was a busy time.

"I can think of no better time to do so," Calder said. "There are four beds which I will have delivered tomorrow and set up wherever you need them."

Mrs. Armstrong blinked at him. "I— Thank you, Your Grace. I am overcome by your generosity."

"I apologize it has taken me so long to determine how I might continue the support my father offered."

Felicity heard the faint note of distaste when he said "my father," but doubted Mrs. Armstrong would have heard it. It took everything Felicity had not to take his hand and give him a reassuring squeeze.

"I am exceedingly grateful, Your Grace. May I offer you refreshment? Or a tour?"

"I must be on my way, but if you could provide a list of things you require, I will see about fulfilling it. I would also like an itemization of the repairs you are aware of and will provide it to the architectural firm I hire in London next month."

"You're going to hire a firm?" Mrs. Armstrong looked as if she needed to sit down.

"Of course. I am not an expert on such matters."

That would be very expensive. Clearly, money had never been the issue when it came to Calder's miserliness. Felicity's heart ached to hear it, but she knew he was making changes for the better, that he was finding his way back.

Mrs. Armstrong shook her head. "Thank you. Lord Darlington will be so thrilled. I imagine he already knows, since he's your brother-in-law." She smiled. "And now I'm just blathering."

"Mrs. Armstrong?"

The call came from the kitchen, prompting Mrs. Armstrong to look in that direction. "If you'll excuse me." She gave Calder a final broad grin. "Thank you so much."

When she was gone, Felicity turned to him. "I want to say I'm surprised, but this is precisely what the Calder I know would do. I'm so glad you found him."

His features darkened for a moment. "I had to get you to stop bothering me."

"Oh, is that it?" Felicity put a hand on her hip. "Perhaps you'd like to explain why Alice hugged you? That is the part that has me surprised. No, it has me incredulous."

He waved his hand. "I provided her with a little direction, nothing more."

"Regarding how to exact revenge on Freddie?"

Calder exhaled with exasperation, his gaze at last meeting Felicity's. "He kept stealing her biscuits and pulling her hair."

Felicity smothered a grin. "And how were you even aware of his shenanigans?"

"I came yesterday to see things for myself. Because someone"—he glowered at her—"kept pestering me. I met Alice, and she required my assistance."

"How did you do it?" Felicity edged closer to him, looking up at him with rapt interest.

"My cook prepared biscuits that were intended to be stolen. They were, ah, infested with some sort of vermin."

That explained Freddie's screaming and spitting while hopping around. "I want to feel bad for him," Felicity said, smiling in spite of herself, "but I suppose no harm was done."

"None at all, and it was an important lesson— mostly the humiliation in front of his peers. He won't bother Alice again."

Felicity had a horrid thought. Had Calder's father done this to him? "Please tell me you don't know this from experience."

"No. I would have preferred humiliation in front of my peers to what was—" He clenched his jaw. "Never mind."

She took his hand then and gave him the squeeze she'd been longing to give. "I'm so sorry, Calder. All that is behind you now."

His eyes were sad, desperate almost, and her heart bled. "I want it to be, but sometimes I just don't know." He pulled his hand away. "I need to go."

She wanted him to stay, but to what end? So she could hold him and soothe him? This was neither the place nor the time. "Are the beds you're delivering from my father's house?"

Calder nodded. "Unless you mind?"

She shook her head. "Not at all. I suggested it, after all. I'm delighted you're giving them to Hartwell House. You've a good heart, despite your best efforts to the contrary." She said this with dry humor, but he didn't smile. Those were still few and far between where he was concerned. Perhaps Felicity would ask Alice for her secret in eliciting smiles, laughter, and hugs from the Duke of Hartwell.

"Felicity, you would do well to remember that I don't try to have a black heart—that's simply the way it is. The sooner you realize that, the better off you will be. And maybe then you'll stop bothering me."

He strode from the room, leaving her to stare after him in sad confusion. She'd been certain he was making progress.

Perhaps he was referring to them. Just because he was hosting St. Stephen's Day and supporting Hartwell House didn't mean he was ready to open himself up to personal relationships—to love. To heartache.

Because Felicity knew that with love came heartache. For her, she would gladly risk the latter to have the former. She just wasn't sure Calder would ever be able to share that sentiment.

CHAPTER 8

A light dusting of snow covered the ground on Christmas Eve morning when Calder set out with his sisters and brothers-in-law to find the Yule log. They were all on horseback, while a groom drove a wagon that would convey the tree back to the house. Isis ran alongside Calder.

The sensation of being with his sisters and their husbands was odd, probably because it was the first time. He'd only been back at Hartwell since last spring, and it had been years before that. He felt as though he barely knew them.

"This is a nice copse of trees," Poppy said. "Let's look here."

Her husband quickly dismounted and hurried to help her. He lifted her from the horse very carefully and set her gently on the ground.

Calder didn't particularly care about the Yule log. Before he'd agreed to allow his sisters to come, he hadn't even planned on finding one. The only reason he'd joined them today was to get out with Isis, who loved the snow. He climbed down from his horse, and Isis ran to his side.

"Did we get a Yule log from this copse once?" Bianca asked.

"You've a good memory," Poppy said. "You couldn't have been more than five or so."

That would have made Calder thirteen. He'd been home from Eton, though he would have preferred to remain at school.

They walked as a group toward the trees, surveying them as they went. Everyone but Calder. They could find an old, rotting log on the ground, and that would be fine with him.

"Thank you for inviting us to Hartwell," Buckleigh said. "I'm glad to put the past behind us. Hopefully you are too."

"Ash," Bianca hissed before nudging her husband in the ribs. "Not now."

"Sorry," Buckleigh murmured.

"Now is fine," Calder said, exhaling. "I plan to give Bianca her settlement."

Poppy stepped toward him and touched his arm, smiling. "Thank you."

If he'd been uncomfortable in the face of Mrs. Armstrong's gratitude, this was ten times worse. He felt as if he wanted to crawl out of his skin. He pointed at a tree. "How about that one?"

"Too skinny," Bianca said.

She was right, but then Calder hadn't really looked at it. He'd just been trying to divert the conversation.

Bianca moved toward the one beside it. "This one. It's perfect."

"It is," Poppy agreed. They both looked to Calder, who shrugged. "Gabriel?" Poppy asked.

"Whatever my love desires." Darlington gazed at her with warmth and love, and though Calder tried to remain immune, his insides twisted with envy.

"I'll fetch the axe," Buckleigh said, going back to the wagon.

Bianca walked over to Calder. "This is really starting to feel like Christmas. I'm so glad we're all here together." Her bright blue eyes sparkled in the morning sunlight filtering through the clouds.

Poppy stepped beside her and linked her arm through Bianca's. "Yes, and just think, next year, there will be little footprints in the snow."

Bianca laughed. "Unless your child learns to walk at an alarmingly young age, I should think not."

Poppy giggled, and now Calder understood why Darlington had handled her with such care.

Again, he felt a pang of envy. "Congratulations."

"Thank you," Poppy said. "I know you aren't aware, and why should you be, but I'd believed I couldn't have children. Gabriel and I have been married nearly three years and... Well, we are very happy."

A warm sensation sprouted in Calder's chest, then spread outward. Happiness—not for him, but for his sister, who was the kindest soul he'd ever known. If anyone deserved the joy of a child, it was her. "I'm glad for you," he said quietly.

Poppy turned her head and wiped a finger over her eye. "I wish Papa was here to share in our happiness."

And just like that, the faint flame inside Calder sputtered and died. "I don't." The words fell from his mouth unbidden, and he immediately wished he could take them back.

Of course, Bianca asked, "Why didn't you like him? He was so distraught that you never came to visit, especially at the end."

Calder couldn't tell them. They ought to go their entire lives without knowing how cruel he'd been.

He focused on Buckleigh, who'd returned with

the axe. He and Darlington were discussing how to take down the tree. The footman stood nearby, ready to offer assistance. Calder would help too. He'd rip the damn thing from the ground in order to avoid this conversation with his sisters.

But before he could walk away, Bianca said, "Do you remember the Yule log that nearly set the house on fire?"

Poppy's eyes widened. "Yes! That was almost a disaster." She looked over at Calder. "Were you there that year?"

Calder had missed a few Christmases due to accepting invitations from friends at school. He didn't recall the fire. "I don't think so."

"My favorite part of finding the Yule log was Papa singing," Bianca said, smiling. "He had such a nice voice—which you inherited," she said to Poppy. "I could carry that tree better than I could a tune."

They both laughed, and suddenly, Calder couldn't stand listening to their fond memories of "Papa" a moment longer. Something inside him splintered and blew apart, like artillery that had jammed instead of firing cleanly as it was intended to. Calder was supposed to suffer his father in silence. But then that was what the man had wanted, wasn't it? Shouldn't Calder want to do the opposite, as he'd done with everything else?

He stared at them. "Here's a memory that neither of you likely remember. In fact, I believe Bianca was just a baby. Yes, that's right, because the year after Mama died was the very worst. And Poppy, you too would have been at home with the nurse."

Both his sisters looked at him, their gazes a combination of wariness and keen interest.

"We went on the Yule log hunt as always, except

it wasn't the same without Mama. She's the one who sang, and she brought biscuits and a jug of wassail. I'd finally been allowed to drink it the last year she came with us." He couldn't help but look at Bianca, who'd never known the beautiful, vibrant woman who'd been their mother. When he thought of all the pain he'd endured, he knew hers was probably far greater. And yet, he wondered if it was better to have not known her at all than to miss what you could never have again. He'd thought the same thing about Felicity—that he would have been better off if he'd never known her.

"I don't really remember her," Poppy said softly. "I recall her smell—honeysuckle. But everything else, I knew from you." She looked at Calder. "I don't think I ever thanked you for keeping her memory alive for me."

Calder was nearly undone. Because he hadn't done it for her. He'd done it for himself. He was as selfish as one could be, just as his father had said.

"Calder, you were going to tell us about a Yule log hunt," Bianca prompted.

He would have abandoned it after what Poppy had said. But Bianca would press... And the story wanted to be told after all this time. "I chose a tree, but he said it wasn't right. It was too... I don't even remember." Calder stared past them into the distance, that day as clear in his mind as the landscape before him. "I really wanted that tree. It reminded me of the one Mama had chosen the year before. I just knew it was the one she would have wanted. But he wouldn't allow it, and because I argued, he left me there."

"Where?" Poppy whispered, her eyes wide with alarm.

Calder shrugged. "Far from the house. It took

me hours to find my way home. And it had started snowing. I was near freezing, and when I got there, all he could do was tell me not to drip on the carpet."

"Oh my God," Bianca breathed, moving close to his side while Poppy came up on the other.

"Did he do other things like that?" Poppy asked, her voice barely more than a croak.

"All the time." Calder couldn't look at them. "He treated me very differently than he treated you. And he was always careful to never to let you see." Now he glanced down at Bianca, who stared at him, her eyes sad. "I expected you—especially—to say it couldn't be true."

"I want to, if only because I don't want to think of him treating you like that, but I can see that he did."

She did? Yes, he heard the anguish in her voice.

"Oh, Calder, I wish you'd told us." Poppy slipped her arm around his back and laid her head on his arm. It was an attempt at a hug, but he was frozen, locked in the past.

"I didn't want you to know."

"Your pride is ridiculous," Bianca said gently, clasping his hand.

He pulled away from both of them. "It wasn't my pride! It was *him*. You loved him. He loved you both. He gave you the best of himself. I lost the only parent who cared for me, and when he lost her, I bore the brunt of his emotions. Nothing I did was ever good enough. He couldn't even let me have the woman I loved." Maybe now they would understand why he chose not to feel. Nothing good came of it.

Poppy moved first, taking a step toward him. "I'm so sorry."

Everything blurred. He didn't want their pity. He didn't want anything.

Turning, he stalked from the copse. Isis followed him, looking up in curiosity as he mounted his horse. "Stay," Calder said, knowing the others would take her back to the house with them. Right now, he wasn't sure where he was going. Or, frankly, if he was coming back.

∾

*T*hankfully, the snow hadn't been too thick upon the ground, or Felicity would not have been able to travel to her old family cottage. She hadn't returned to see it in its entirety, and she wanted to do so before the beds were taken away today.

She arrived early, just as footmen and grooms from Hartwood arrived. She helped direct them, and wondered why Calder wasn't there. They'd told her that he was on a Yule log hunt with his family.

Now, as they loaded up the last of the beds, she was still smiling. It seemed Calder had truly come a long way. Maybe he was finally ready to let the past go and look to a brighter future.

One of the footmen came to speak with her in the entry hall. "We're ready to go to Hartwell House. Thank you for your assistance, Mrs. Garland."

"It was my pleasure. Happy Christmas to you."

"And to you. Will we see you on St. Stephen's Day?"

"I expect so. I wouldn't miss it."

He inclined his head with a smile, then left. Gathering her shawl around her shoulders, Felicity closed the door behind him before going upstairs to douse the small fire she'd built in the sitting room. While the footmen and grooms had moved furniture, she'd taken her ease in a chair that she hoped Calder would allow her to take home. She'd ask him later, maybe on St. Stephen's Day, since that was likely the next time she'd see him.

A creak in the floorboard drew her to turn from the doorway to the sitting room. Calder stood at the top of the stairs.

He wore no hat or gloves, and he was in the process of removing his greatcoat, which he dropped to the floor. He ran his hand through his dark hair, standing the thick strands on end. His gray eyes, usually so cold and aloof, were ablaze, like liquid silver. Something was very wrong.

She went to him and took his hands in hers. He wasn't as cold as she'd expected him to be, but he was still chilled. "You need a fire. There's one burning in the hearth in the sitting room."

He shook his head. "I just need you."

Oh. A current of desire rushed through her. The sensation was like nothing she'd ever experienced, and yet she recognized it immediately.

She slid her hands up his front and curled them around the lapels of his coat. Her shawl fell to the floor behind her. "Tell me how."

"Any way you'll let me."

She didn't know what had happened on their Yule log hunt to send him here in a desperate frenzy, and she wasn't sure it mattered. She was just glad she'd been here to meet him. At last, something had worked in their favor, bringing them together instead of pushing them apart.

"I'm here. I'm yours."

He clasped his arms around her and kissed her, his mouth crashing into hers. This wasn't the curious, eager kisses of their youth, nor was it the somewhat cautious kisses from the other day. This was fire and ice, the absolute extreme of kisses. Felicity felt she might wither and die if it didn't continue, if they weren't allowed to see this through to whatever end they both wanted.

Only, she didn't want an end. She wanted forever.

His lips and tongue moved with hers as if the last decade had never come between them, as if they'd been made for each other. She'd certainly thought that was true ten years ago. She fervently hoped it was true now.

His hands moved up her back and plucked at the pins in her hair, sending them cascading to the floor. Then his fingers were sifting through her curls, massaging her scalp and palming her head as he devoured her mouth.

She pulled away with a gasp, then took his hand and pulled him to the sitting room where she'd learned to stitch and write and so many other things. He allowed her to lead him to the fireplace, then he tugged her against him and kissed her once more, leaving no doubt as to what he intended. Good, because if he tried to walk away from her now, she might bring down the house around them to make him stay.

He loosened the ties at the back of her dress, and in response, she tugged his cravat until the knot came undone. They spent the next several minutes alternately kissing and removing their clothing until she stood before him in her stays and chemise and he in his shirt and breeches.

"It's cold," she said, wondering if that was why he hesitated to finish undressing.

"I'm not cold. I don't think that's possible when I'm with you. I'm just...savoring this moment. I've

waited so long to touch you like this, to see you...
I've dreamed of it a thousand times."

His words broke her heart yet also somehow
repaired the cracks and holes that she'd learned to
live with. She pulled at the laces on her stays—glad
that these were in the front—her gaze locked with
his. "You don't have to wait anymore. And this isn't
a dream."

Loose, the stays sagged around her rib cage. She
pushed them over her hips and down her legs until
they hit the floor. Then she gently kicked them to
the side.

Reaching for the hem of her chemise, she
clasped the cotton firmly before tugging it over her
head. She stood before him completely bare, something she'd never done with her husband. Their in-
timacy had always happened in the darkness, and
she'd always worn her night rail. Just standing here
exposed to him was the most erotic thing she'd
ever done.

If it were anyone else, she might have been shy,
but this was Calder. Her heart. Her soul. And he
looked at her as if she were a goddess—*his* goddess.
She'd never seen anything more alluring than the
possession and hunger heating his gaze.

"You're even more beautiful than I imagined,"
he whispered, moving closer to her. He stroked the
side of her face, his fingers gliding over her flesh,
down her throat, gently caressing her collarbone.
Then lower still until his hand moved over her
breast. The contact of his skin against hers coaxed
a moan from her throat. She felt utterly brazen as
she pushed herself toward him, seeking more of
his touch.

He seemed to know what she wanted, for he
cupped her, softly at first, and then more firmly,
his fingers closing over her nipple and giving it a

gentle tug. He did the same with her other breast, both of his hands moving over her, arousing her, driving a sweet and desperate desire straight to her sex.

He pulled on her nipples in concert, and she gasped. Then he dipped his head and took one of them in his mouth, sucking on her. The sensation made her knees buckle as another wave of hunger shot through her.

He wrapped his arm around her and led her to the settee, which was only a foot away and situated in front of the fire. Guiding her down, he laid her back, then knelt on the floor beside her.

She looked at him in question, wondering why he was on the floor and not climbing on top of her. "What are you doing?"

"Worshipping you," he said simply before dropping his head to her breast once more. He cupped her, holding her flesh captive to his questing lips and tongue. And teeth—he nipped at her and she bucked up in surprise and pleasure.

As his hand trailed down her abdomen, she was aware of a throbbing need between her legs. She'd felt a similar sensation before, but nothing like this ache that begged to be satisfied. She squirmed, eager for something that she knew had always been just beyond her reach.

She cried out as his fingers skimmed across her sex.

"Part your legs, Felicity," he urged softly.

She followed his command, ready for whatever he would do and hoping this time would be different. It had to be—this was Calder. He stroked a spot at the top of her sex, and her body twitched with pleasure.

She closed her eyes and lost herself in his touch. "Oh yes. Oh yes. Oh yes." She couldn't seem to stop herself from saying that over and over.

He slipped one of his fingers into her and thrust deep, filling her. She whimpered and moved her hips, wanting more. He gave it to her, sliding in and out while his thumb continued to work that glorious spot.

His other hand cupped the back of her neck and turned her head to face him. "Open your eyes, love," he whispered. "I want you to look at me when I bring you to orgasm."

She did as he bade, his hand supporting her head as she looked into his silvery eyes. When he came into her next, there was more—two fingers, perhaps—and she cried out. Her eyes tried to close, but his fingers dug into her neck. "Look at me, Felicity."

He drove into her again and again, filling her, bringing her to a dizzying height. "God, you're beautiful. I can't—" He broke eye contact and moved his head down her body. Then his mouth was on her there, licking and sucking at her flesh as his fingers continued their wild, delicious penetration.

She couldn't keep her eyes open as she was overcome by a pleasure so great that it seemed as if she were flung into a dark night sky studded with brilliant stars. She floated there in absolute ecstasy. Until she fell. A glorious, spectacular fall that made her body shudder and her heart sing.

When she at last opened her eyes, she saw Calder sitting back on his feet, his breathing loud and fast, his eyes dilated as he gazed at her body. "I want to see you," she said, turning and sliding from the settee.

She knelt before him and found the hem of his shirt. He said nothing, just stared at her, his face tense, his body taut. She saw just how taut as she pulled the garment over his head. The muscles of his shoulders and chest were clearly defined, showing him to be an athletic man. She caressed his collarbones and drew her hands down his front, skimming her palms over his warm flesh so she could memorize every dip and plane.

As her hands moved lower, he sucked in a breath, holding it. "Is something wrong?" she asked softly, her hands pausing.

"No. Don't stop."

She trailed her fingers down to the waistband of his breeches. "How am I to undress you with you sitting like that?"

In a flash, he stood and divested himself of his remaining garments. As he knelt back down, she stared at his sex. She'd never looked at her husband's—never mind, she didn't want to think of anything but Calder.

Curious, she reached for him, then hesitated. "May I?" she asked shyly.

"Please." He took her hand and curled it around his shaft. "My cock would like nothing better than for you to touch it."

Cock. That word was both crude and incredibly arousing. She decided she would like nothing better than to touch it. "Show me," she said.

He kept his hand on hers and moved hers down to the base. "Stroke me. Not too hard. Not too soft." He looked at her intently, his hand guiding hers.

She did as he described, clasping his flesh with a firm grip and gliding her palm up and down. She found moisture at the tip, and, curious, she ran her thumb over it.

He groaned. "Felicity, get on the settee."

She started to rise, and he helped her, all but

lifting her and laying her on her back. "I'm sorry there aren't any beds," she said, smiling.

"I wouldn't even need a settee." He covered her with his body and kissed her deeply, his tongue driving deep into her mouth as his hand found her sex once more.

She opened her legs, and he settled between them—as best as the settee would allow them—his cock pushing at her entrance. Desire pulsed from her sex and outward. She wanted that...orgasm again. Could she have it again? It certainly felt as if she could.

He slid into her, kissing her neck, as she stretched to accommodate him, her body welcoming him as if he'd come home at last. And she supposed he had.

He moved slowly, filling her, then retreating, then gradually filling her again. It felt divine and yet it was nowhere near enough. She clasped his backside, urging him to move faster. "Please, Calder."

Then he let go. His mouth claimed hers briefly as he drove into her. She groaned, digging her fingers into his flesh, desperate for the rapture spiraling through her. She moved with him, their bodies finding a rhythm that pushed her to the edge once more. She looked out over the inky sky with this carpet of stars and dove headfirst into sweet oblivion. Her body crashed and exploded beneath his, then she felt him stiffen. He called out her name, then shouted over and over as he thrust deep inside her.

A lethargy so complete and so wondrous fell over her. He turned with her, holding her close so she was pinned between him and the back of the settee. Smiling, she nestled against him, happier than she could ever remember being.

Gradually, their breathing evened, and his became steady and deep. She opened her eyes the barest amount and surmised that he'd dozed off. Content, she kissed his jaw and whispered, "I love you."

Then she joined him in slumber.

CHAPTER 9

*W*hy was it so bloody cold?

His skin felt like ice, as if he'd never be warm again. Mist swirled around him, prompting him to wonder how it was already night and how he'd gotten outside.

The mist faded. He wasn't outside. Before him was a cozy sitting room filled with people he didn't recognize. No, that wasn't quite true. The woman standing near the hearth was utterly familiar—her green eyes alight with joy as she took the hand of the man who came to join her.

His hair was gray and hers was white. The others were younger, and one woman was clearly their daughter. A child clutched at her skirt, and the woman swept her into her arms then carried her to the green-eyed woman—Felicity.

She smiled at the girl. "Happy Christmas, my sweet."

"Grandmama!" The child reached for her, and Felicity welcomed her into her arms. "Grandpapa!" She grinned at the man beside Felicity.

He chuckled softly, his eyes so full of love and pride, it tore at Calder's chest. What sorcery was this? Felicity's hair was blonde. Her husband was dead. She wasn't a mother, let alone a grandmother.

And what was the pine tree, candles flickering on its limbs, standing in the corner, some sort of Yule log abomination? "That's going to catch the house on fire!" Calder called out.

No one seemed to hear him. He moved forward and waved his hand in front of Felicity's face. Her attention didn't waver from her granddaughter.

Granddaughter... They all looked so happy. And where was he? Why wasn't he there?

The mist returned, as did the icy cold. When the air next cleared, he remained outside. The sky above was gray, and around him, headstones rose from the dormant grass.

The drone of a voice carried on the wind. Calder walked between the stones, his heart pounding. A small gathering stood over a hole in the ground. The vicar finished speaking, then looked to those standing around the perimeter. Just four people—his sisters and their husbands.

Like Felicity, they looked older. Their hair was gray, and lines around their eyes showed their age.

He moved to the hole and looked down at the simple wood coffin. "Who died?" he asked.

As with Felicity and her family, none of them reacted to his presence. They neither saw nor heard him.

"I hope he's at peace now," Poppy said, looking sadly down into the hole. She turned her head toward Bianca. "I can't believe there's no heir anywhere. After all these generations, there will be no Staffords at Hartwood. What will even become of Hartwood?" Poppy looked at her husband.

The marquess shrugged. "The queen will decide."

Queen? There was a queen? What bloody year was this?

"It's such a mess anyway," Bianca said, frowning. "I can't believe how badly Calder let it decline before he died."

It was him in the hole. Calder began to shake. He hadn't thought he could feel colder, but he did.

"It's not as if he kept a reasonable number of retainers," Bianca's husband said. "Those he did have never stayed long, and can you blame them?"

Poppy shook her head. "No, he was absolutely horrid."

"Terrifying, actually." Bianca shuddered. "Last time I saw him—over a year ago—what was left of his gray hair reached to the middle of his back. He could barely focus his eyes, and his hands were like claws."

"Well, he always was a beast," Darlington murmured. "Sorry," he added, placing his hand on Poppy's back and offering her a sympathetic smile.

"He had only himself to blame, that's true," Poppy said with a sigh.

"He died alone just as he chose to live his life." Bianca shook her head with pity.

Poppy looked toward the young vicar. "Please say an extra prayer for our brother tonight."

"I will, my lady."

After a final look into the hole, Bianca turned away. Poppy's mouth pitched down before she pivoted and put her arm through her sister's. They walked from the grave together, their husbands trailing behind.

The vicar gestured toward the gravediggers. The two men came forward with their shovels and began to fill in the hole.

As the dirt hit the wood, the outside world around Calder disappeared. Now there was nothing but blackness and a stifling smell of cut wood and dank. A steady tap-tap sounded above him. It was like rain, but not. He reached out, and his hands struck wood right in front of him.

He was in the coffin.

He pounded on the wood, screaming, his hands be-

coming battered and bruised. He couldn't be dead. Not now, not after what he'd just found...

The wood beneath him gave way, and he inexplicably fell. Into an abyss...

"Calder, wake up!"

He pushed forward again, expecting to find a barrier. There was nothing. He opened his eyes in panic to see where he'd fallen.

"Calder!"

A voice he knew. Her voice. He blinked and saw Felicity's youthful, unlined face and her golden-blonde hair. Lifting his head, he looked around in confusion, then recognized the sitting room in her family's cottage.

She was naked, as was he. Then he remembered. They'd been on the settee. "Did I fall asleep?" he asked.

"Yes, we dozed for a while. You started screaming, and then you fell to the floor."

He'd fallen to the *floor*.

He dropped his head back onto the rug and stared up at the ceiling as he gulped deep breaths to calm his racing pulse. It had been a dream. He'd been dead and his family hadn't seemed to care, though he supposed it was enough that they'd come to his grave. Even if they hadn't shed a tear? They'd sounded relieved. And disappointed—he'd let them and the dukedom down.

Then there was Felicity. Happy with her large family, including her husband, who obviously adored her. Calder squeezed his eyes closed to banish the image from his mind, but feared it was emblazoned in his memory forever.

"We should get dressed," Felicity said.

He opened his eyes to see her rising. She went about collecting their clothing and set the garments on the settee. Calder dressed quickly, which

Felicity couldn't possibly do. He itched to leave, to flee, but he forced himself to stay, to help her.

After he had her dress laced, he looked toward the door. "I need to go."

"Yes, I must get home to my mother." She sat down on the settee to don her boots. "Where do you need to be?"

Anywhere but here. He walked toward the door.

"Calder, did you hear me?"

He paused at the threshold. "Felicity, you must forget about me. You deserve a long and happy life." The one he'd seen for her. The one he obviously couldn't give her.

She stood, her brow furrowing with deep creases as she frowned. "I could never forget about you. Not if a thousand years passed."

Her words flayed him. There was nothing he could do to change who he was, who he was destined to be. That dream had been the future, and their paths separated most severely. It was as it should be.

He gave her his most frigid stare. "I am not the man you think I am."

"You're the man I love," she said simply, walking toward him.

Her declaration nearly drove him to his knees. Love was not an emotion he knew or understood outside of the context of loss. He'd loved his mother. He'd loved Felicity. He'd tried to love his sisters but, because of his father, had never felt they were his to love.

"I shouldn't be, Felicity, and it's time you understood that."

She rushed forward and clasped his hand. "I love the man whose best friend is a dog, who helps a little girl in her time of need, who would hire an expensive architecture firm to repair an old, drafty manor house so it can become a school for impoverished children."

Aside from Isis, none of that was really him. It was *her* influence. He pulled his hand from hers and drew himself up with forced contempt. "Ten years ago, I lost the only thing that mattered to me, then I spent the next few years losing everything else. When I couldn't sink any lower, my father kicked me—he took away his support and told me to sort myself out. I was broke and alone. I took the only thing of value I had left—my mother's jewels—and I sold them. From that, I have built everything that I am today. My father wasn't good with money. If not for me, there actually wouldn't be funds to support Hartwell House at all. There would barely be enough to pay Bianca's settlement." He'd never said those things to anyone, and now they flew from his mouth like caged birds free for the first time.

She gaped at him, her jaw open and her eyes round. "Calder, those days are behind you now. Your father isn't here. He doesn't matter."

"He will always matter! We are the Dukes of Hartwell! Beholden to our legacy of stern leadership and rigid duty." He'd never felt more encumbered. The boards of the coffin closed in around him.

Unable to bear the light of her presence another moment, Calder turned and stalked from the sitting room, pausing only to retrieve his greatcoat from the top of the stairs.

Outside, he paused, wondering how Felicity had gotten there and how she would return home. Though it wasn't yet midafternoon, it was still bitterly cold, particularly with the wind. Then he saw the stable with its telltale curl of smoke coming from the chimney and her vehicle outside. The coachman and horse had to be inside, which meant Calder didn't have to worry about her.

Not that he wouldn't.

He would care about her, want her, *love* her for the rest of his days. Until he was cold in the ground in that unforgiving wooden box.

~

*F*elicity rushed downstairs and watched Calder hesitate outside. Had he changed his mind?

She ran to the door just as he strode to his horse. He mounted, and she called out his name. Either he didn't hear her, or he was pretending not to, for he raced away.

Distraught, she turned and went back into the house. She trudged back upstairs to douse the fire in the sitting room, which she'd intended to do hours ago. Oh dear, what must the coachman think? She'd quite lost track of...everything the moment Calder had taken her into his arms.

Then they'd slept, their bodies entwined. She wasn't sure she'd ever known such joy, such peace. When he'd awakened her screaming, the sound had driven terror deep into her heart.

His eyes had been wild, his heart beating frantically. She suspected he'd had a nightmare—what else could explain his behavior when she'd roused him from sleep?

And what had he dreamed that had scared him so terribly? That had driven him not just from the house, but from her, seemingly forever? He'd told her to forget about him. As she'd responded, she wouldn't do that. She *couldn't*.

She wasn't going to let him get away.

After taking care of the fire, she went to gather

her cloak, hat, and gloves. Once she was bundled up, she went to the stable and notified the coachman she was ready to depart.

"I'll just be a few minutes, ma'am," he said.

"We aren't going home. We're going to Hartwood."

He inclined his head. "Aye, Mrs. Garland."

When they arrived at Hartwood, Felicity had a bad feeling he wasn't there. She rapped on the door as nervous energy coursed through her.

The butler, Truro, answered, his eyes warming when he saw her. "What a pleasure to see you again, Mrs. Garland. Happy Christmas."

"Happy Christmas to you too. I'm here to see His Grace."

A small pucker gathered between Truro's sherry-colored eyes. "I'm afraid he isn't at home. Would you care to see Lady Darlington or Lady Buckleigh?"

"Yes, please," Felicity answered with far too much zeal.

Truro showed her to the drawing room, then took her cloak, hat, and gloves. She went to the fireplace to warm herself, but she was so anxious, she ended up pacing in front of the hearth.

"Felicity?" Bianca came into the drawing room with Poppy following behind her.

Felicity stopped and faced them. "I'm sorry to intrude on Christmas Eve, but I'm concerned about Calder."

"So are we," Bianca said, frowning.

That only increased Felicity's alarm. "What happened?"

"We were on the Yule log hunt," Poppy said, her features creased with worry. "He shared some"— she glanced at her sister—"things."

Felicity had been shocked he'd gone with them,

but she was even more surprised that he'd shared anything with them. "What things?" She couldn't help but wonder if they were related to his nightmare. Or the state in which he'd arrived at the house. He'd been disoriented, adrift, as if he were looking for something—or someone—to hang on to.

"About our father," Poppy said. She moved closer to Bianca and took her hand. "He was quite awful to Calder. We never knew."

Felicity could understand how they felt. When she'd learned her father had taken money from Calder's father, she'd wondered if she'd ever known him at all. "He paid my father to take us and leave Hartwell so that Calder and I wouldn't wed. He told Calder I'd greedily taken the money and gladly avoided marriage to him. Then he sent me a forged letter from Calder telling me we would never suit, that I wasn't worthy of becoming his duchess."

Both sisters' eyes widened, and their clasped hands fell apart. Poppy lifted her hand to her mouth, while Bianca clenched her jaw.

"That's why you left," Bianca said with enough disdain to fill a moat. "If not for our father, you and Calder would have been married these past ten years."

"Oh, Felicity, that's just—" Poppy's voice caught. She blinked several times before she could continue. "I'm so sorry."

"Thank you, but it's in the past, and we can't change what happened. All we can do is help Calder be the man he wants to be, the man he is deep down, the man I fell in love with." She looked at them both intently. "The man I still love."

Bianca grinned. "I'm so glad to hear that. Also, I knew it." She slid Poppy a triumphant glance.

Poppy looked as though she wanted to hug Felicity, but then her smile faded. "Why are you concerned about him?"

"He was with me—after your Yule log hunt, I would surmise."

"He left rather abruptly," Bianca said. "He seemed overwhelmed."

"And not in a good way." Poppy's tone was dark. "How was he with you?"

"Upset, but then...better." She tried to find a word that would accurately describe his mood without giving away too much. They didn't need to know the specifics. "When he left, he was upset again—more so than when he'd arrived. He told me to forget about him." It hurt to remember him saying it, but it was even more painful to repeat the words aloud to his sisters.

"Clearly, that's not going to happen," Bianca said briskly. "Where do we think he went?"

Felicity shook her head. "I can't begin to imagine." She would have thought the very house where they'd been, since she'd found him there the other day. Beyond that, she had no inkling where he might go. She considered the meadow where they'd had their picnic—yes, she'd look there.

"What about Papa's folly?" Poppy asked, looking to Bianca. Then she flinched. "I can't help feeling betrayed every time I think of him now," she said with soft anguish.

Bianca nodded, her mouth tight. "When I consider all the time I nursed him when he was ill, all the things he said in disappointment about Calder, not one word of praise or love. I never stopped to ask why. I just accepted that Calder was cold and unfeeling. It didn't occur to me to determine *why* he was that way." Bianca's voice broke. She pressed a finger to the corner of her eye. A tear fell anyway, and she wiped it away.

"None of us did, at least not enough to actually help him." Poppy's tone weighed heavy with regret. "We are as much to blame as our father."

"So is Calder," Felicity said. "He chooses to be this way because it's easy and familiar. Even now he's trying to please the man he could never satisfy. He says he does the things he does to make his father angry—and at some level, I'm sure he does. However, he's still waiting for the approval that will never come."

"That all makes such sense." Poppy wrapped her arms around herself. "What can we do?"

Felicity looked from one sister to the other. "We have to find him."

"You don't think he'll come back of his own accord?" Bianca asked.

"I don't know. He was extremely troubled." Felicity glanced out the window and saw the flutter of snowflakes drifting every now and again. "Unfortunately, I must return home to see to my mother." Agatha was with her now, but it was Christmas Eve, and she needed to get home to her family.

"You should fetch her and come back," Poppy said. "Gabriel will go with you and help you with whatever you need."

"Are you sure it won't be an inconvenience if we come?" Felicity wasn't sure how she was going to describe all this to her mother. She hadn't discussed Calder with her at all. A part of Felicity was still hurt because of the role her mother had played in keeping the truth from Felicity the past decade.

Bianca waved her hand. "Of course it's not an inconvenience. This is where you belong, especially on Christmas. You're family." She smiled. "Or you will be as soon as you and Calder wed."

Felicity wasn't sure that would come to pass, not after what he'd said. But after everything else that had transpired since she'd returned, she'd never wanted anything more. "I'll be back as soon as I can."

"We'll start the search immediately." Bianca moved toward her and took her hand. "We'll find him."

Poppy came and clasped Felicity's other hand. "We aren't going to lose him now, not when we've finally found him. He needs us, and we won't let him down."

Yes, he needed them, and Felicity would move heaven and earth to get to him.

CHAPTER 10

*F*elicity returned to Hartwood with her mother in a remarkably short amount of time. Retainers had already begun to look for Calder around the estate, and Ash and Bianca had gone to the folly that the former duke had built.

After settling her mother in with Poppy, whom Gabriel insisted remain at the house given her condition and the fact that it was now fully snowing, Felicity prepared to ride out with Gabriel. Isis whined from her spot in front of the hearth in the drawing room.

"Why isn't she out looking?" Felicity asked, thinking that if anyone would find him, it would be his beloved dog.

"I'm not sure, but she can come with us."

"She needs her coat." Felicity went in search of Truro, who helped her prepare Isis for their excursion.

As they walked toward the stable, Felicity shared her only idea as to his location. "I want to look in a meadow. It's northeast of here." The ride was probably a mile and a half, just past that edge of the estate's property.

"Lead the way," Gabriel said.

They rode swiftly, with Isis easily keeping pace, and thankfully, the snow let up until they'd nearly reached the meadow. The grass was white, and it was coldly beautiful—so very different from the day she'd spent here with Calder.

Bringing his horse to a stop next to Felicity, Gabriel looked about. "I don't see anyone."

"Look." Felicity pointed to Isis, who had paused with them and was now trotting toward a stand of trees. The trot became a run as she drew closer.

Felicity kicked her horse after the dog and heard Gabriel follow behind her. Calder's horse stood grazing nearby, on a patch of grass beneath the trees that hadn't been coated with snow.

Felicity searched for Isis and saw the greyhound's tail sticking from behind a tree. Sliding down from her horse, Felicity ran to the dog. Propped against the tree was Calder, his eyes closed, his lips a terrifying gray.

"Calder, wake up!" Felicity knelt beside him and drew off her glove to touch his face. His cheek was like ice. "Calder!"

Isis nudged him and then climbed onto his lap. She laid her head against his chest.

"She's trying to warm him up," Gabriel said. "We need to get him home."

Felicity turned her head to look up at the marquess. "How do we do that?"

"We'll get him onto my horse. I can ride back with him."

Stroking Isis's head, Felicity whispered, "We'll take care of him." She stood and faced Gabriel. "Let's move quickly."

He nodded, then went to fetch the horses. "Can you lead his horse?" he asked Felicity.

"Yes." She tried not to let fear paralyze her. Calder had never needed her more.

It took a great deal of effort, but they got him on Gabriel's horse, and Gabriel climbed on behind him. It was awkward, which made the return trip much slower than Felicity would have liked.

When they arrived at the house, Truro rushed outside to help Gabriel carry Calder inside. A groom came to care for the horses, and Felicity and Isis followed the men into the house.

Poppy stood inside the entry hall. "Where did you find him?"

"A meadow where we once had a picnic," Felicity said. "I'm afraid he's nearly frozen."

"Should we send for Dr. Fisk?" Poppy asked.

"I hate to trouble him on Christmas Eve. I'm sure we can handle things." Felicity sounded calmer than she felt. If Calder took ill, she wasn't sure what she would do. No, she wasn't sure what she would do if she lost him.

She hurried up the stairs and found her way to Calder's bedchamber, where Truro and Gabriel had deposited him on the bed. Calder's valet began undressing him under the watchful eyes of Isis, who sat beside her master. Her gaze held all the love and worry Felicity too possessed.

They got him tucked into the bed, and a pair of maids brought warming pans. A short time later, when Felicity felt his head, her worst fears were confirmed. He was no longer cold but burning hot with fever.

She exchanged a look with Isis. "We aren't going to lose him. I promise."

Isis ducked her head, laying it on Calder's arm. If Calder died, it wouldn't be because no one loved him.

She brushed his hair back from his forehead. "You have so much to fight for," she whispered. "Stay with us. *Please.*"

Then she prayed for a Christmas miracle.

~

*H*e was so cold. His finger and toes were ice. He huddled into himself, but there was simply no heat. Was this how he was going to meet his end? He'd expected to be much older, based on his vision of the future.

But maybe he was. Maybe he'd spent years in a trance, his life nothing but a dark void he couldn't remember. And maybe that was for the best.

Calder opened his eyes and gasped, his body jerking. He blinked, trying to bring the area around him into focus.

There was light and softness and…warmth. There was also movement against his side. That seemed to be the source of the warmth. He reached out and felt the familiar comforting silk of a dog's fur.

"Calder?"

He knew that voice. He blinked several more times until his vision finally became clear. Felicity stood beside his bed, her face splitting into the most relieved smile he'd ever seen.

"What are you doing here?" His voice sounded scratchy, and indeed, his throat felt as if it hadn't been used. Furthermore, his entire body ached. What had happened to him?

Isis nudged the hand he'd placed on her head. Calder looked over and stroked her several times, murmuring, "Good girl."

Felicity smoothed her hand over his forehead and exhaled before smiling even wider. "Your fever has broken."

He'd had a fever? "I was cold."

"I should think so. Isis found you in the

meadow unconscious against a tree." Felicity glanced toward the dog in open admiration. "You were nearly frozen. You took a chill, obviously, and you've had a fever since."

He saw the purple streaks beneath her eyes, the rumpled state of her gown, and the wisps of hair that had escaped her chignon. It was clear she'd been nursing him. "Why are you here taking care of me?"

"Who else should do it? And don't say your valet or a maid or Truro. Of course I would be the one to care for you."

Of course. Only it didn't seem that obvious to him. After the way he'd behaved, she should have run far away—he'd told her to.

Felicity poured water into a glass. "Drink this for your parched throat."

He struggled to sit up, and the room tilted sideways. He closed his eyes briefly while she helped to get him situated against the headboard.

"Ready?" she asked, handing him the glass. He nodded and took a tentative sip, followed by a longer drink.

"You gave us quite a scare." She brushed his hair back from his forehead. "I was with Gabriel. Everyone had spread out to look for you on the estate. I thought you might be in our meadow."

"Isis was with you, apparently." He handed Felicity back the glass, and she set it on the bedside table next to the pitcher. "She is the best friend I've ever had." He stroked the dog's head again and looked at her with love. Yes, love. He knew what that emotion felt like after all. Then he returned his gaze to Felicity. "Next to you."

"How can I possibly be your best friend?" she asked, appearing bemused.

"No one has ever been so persistently dedicated

in their desire to warm my heart. I should say that more than qualifies you."

Felicity laughed softly. "Indeed it does." She perched on the edge of the bed beside him, her thigh next to his. "Why did you run away from me?"

"I was overcome...with emotion." He didn't want to say too much.

"So I understand from your sisters. They told me about the Yule log story you shared with them. About your father." She put her hand on his arm, which was still beneath the covers. "I'd determined some time ago that your father had been particularly cruel to you. One need only look at what he did to us to realize he wasn't kind to you."

"But he was to my sisters. They loved him. They miss him."

"I'm not sure that's the case anymore. They feel terrible that you endured so much without them even realizing."

"I'm six years older than Poppy and eight years older than Bianca. Why would they have realized anything?" Defending them came naturally all of a sudden. He'd seen them as almost enemies since they'd been aligned with the person who was at the core of his misery, but how were they to know how their father had treated him? "I wish I hadn't told them. They deserve to remember him with affection." The way he recalled their mother, whom they couldn't remember at all.

"They are glad to know the truth. They want to help you however they can. *If* they can. They want to be a family." She looked at him sternly. "Before you ran off, you seemed to have had some sort of nightmare. I was terrified for you, and when we couldn't find you... You're a very selfish man, Calder," she said crossly.

He pulled his hand from beneath the covers and laid it over hers. "I am. But I don't want to be. In recent days, I've seen a past I desperately want to reclaim, a present I despise, and a future that terrifies me to my soul."

"Nightmares?" she asked, her beautiful face creasing with concern.

"Sometimes. The past and the present were real. I saw us together, planning to wed. Then my father said that would never happen." There was so much he needed to tell her. But he was so afraid of her reaction. "When you understand how I've lived, the kind of man I became when I thought you rejected me...You'll want to leave."

She put her other hand on top of his, curling her fingers around him. "Never."

"The future I saw—you were there. You were married to someone else. You had children and grandchildren. You were so happy."

"Did my husband look like you?"

He honestly couldn't recall the man's face. "I don't know. But I was dead. My sisters and their husbands—and no one else save a vicar I didn't recognize—came to my burial. I died alone."

"That is not the future, then," she said firmly. "Because I plan to marry only you, and if we're especially blessed, we will have children and grandchildren." She leaned toward him. "And I plan to be so very happy." Her eyes glowed, and he almost believed it.

"When my father said you'd left me, I went to London, where I behaved reprehensibly. I squandered everything—my money, my friendships, my reputation. None of it mattered to me without you. When I learned you'd wed, it only got worse." His voice cracked, and she squeezed his hand between hers. Isis pressed closer against his side. "Then my father cut me off. I awoke one day in a filthy alley outside a gaming hell. I hadn't been able to pay an IOU. Several men thrashed me. That wasn't who I wanted to be. From that moment on, I built myself back up—the money, anyway. And my reputation improved, somewhat." His mouth twisted into a sad smile. "I wasn't known as a wastrel anymore, but an arrogant miser with no interest in joy."

"You quite perfected that," she said with a heavy dash of irony.

"Yes." Miraculously, he chuckled, but it was short-lived. "I've been awful to you. And to my sisters. And to the people of Hartwood and Hartwell."

"You remade yourself once before, I'm confident you can do it again. But this time, you shall be the joyful duke." She fell silent a moment, and he sensed there was a battle being waged behind her eyes. "If you want that."

"Yes, I want that. I'm just not sure I can *be* that."

"I just told you that you could. Do you doubt me?"

"No." He stifled a smile. She was managing him. He rather liked it.

"Do you promise not to run off ever again?"

He looked into her eyes. "I promise."

"Good, because we are in this together. We've lost too much time."

Isis stretched beside him. He turned his head to see her watching him with complete adoration. "I love you too," he murmured to his dog. Then he looked back to Felicity. "But I love you more." Wincing, he glanced back at Isis. "Sorry."

Isis laid her head on his hand. Apparently, she didn't mind.

Felicity cupped his face and stared at him, unblinking. "Did you just say you love me?"

He opened his mouth to repeat himself, but she

kissed him. Then she pulled away, laughing. "I thought it would take months, maybe years, for you to say it. I love you so much, Calder."

"I've no idea why."

She arched a brow at him. "It's very telling when a dog loves someone as much as Isis loves you." She reached over and patted Isis on the head. "And Isis is a very smart dog."

"That she is." He frowned suddenly. "I'm afraid I have no idea what day it is. Did I miss Christmas altogether?"

She nodded. "I'm afraid so. It's St. Stephen's Day."

"It is?" He sat up from the headboard, straightening his spine. "I want to go to the party. Why aren't you there?"

She cocked her head to the side, laughing. "Because I was taking care of you, silly. I don't think you should get out of bed today."

"Sorry, love, but life is too short for me to miss this celebration. The dukes of Hartwell *never* miss it. I'm afraid I'm going, whether you like it or not."

She stood from the bed, her lips set into a deep, disapproving frown. "Fine, but only for a short while, agreed?"

He slipped his legs from the bed and held on to the post as he stood. "I'll agree if you consent to marry me."

"If that was a proposal, it wasn't a very good one. But it doesn't matter. Your sisters and I have already planned the wedding. It's to be at St. Cuthbert's the day after Epiphany."

Yes, she was definitely managing him, and he was absolutely fine with that. "Excellent. I agree. I would be delighted to be your husband."

Laughter, loud and joyous, spilled from her lips.

He joined in, then took her in his arms. She kissed him again, far too briefly. He clasped her more tightly. "Perhaps we could take a few more minutes?"

She stepped back and shook her finger at him. "You're lucky I'm letting you go outside."

Indeed he was. "I'm lucky in every way a man can be," he said quietly, letting her go. "I am yours —happily—to command."

"Let's get you dressed." She gave him a brilliant smile, then walked with him to his dressing chamber.

"I could get used to having you as a valet," he said. Was this really happening? Was she really here with him? He clasped her hand, stopping just as they stepped over the threshold to the dressing room. "Tell me this isn't a dream."

She squeezed his fingers. "It *is*, my love. It's a dream come true."

～

*T*he weather had thankfully warmed on Christmas Day, and the celebration happening on the grounds of Hartwood was a wonder to behold. Large tents housed tables laden with food, barrels of wine and ale, and seating areas for people, especially the old and infirm, to sit and converse. And laugh. Laughter was by far the music of the day.

Pine boughs decorated the tents, as did mistletoe. One of the tents was entirely dedicated to games such as snapdragon. Children spilled from that tent running to and fro, engaging in other games such as Puss in the Corner and Hunt the Fox.

"I want to go speak with Mrs. Armstrong,"

Calder said. She stood laughing between Poppy and Gabriel near one of the games being played.

"Certainly." Felicity had insisted he hold on to her arm the entire time they were outside. He was weak from being abed with fever the past day and a half. Had it only been a day and a half? It had felt like the longest period of her life. She'd been so worried she would lose him. After all the time they'd spent apart and everything he'd been through, it just wouldn't have been fair.

Poppy's eyes lit when she saw Calder and Felicity coming toward them. When they arrived, Calder looked to Felicity and started to take his arm from her. Felicity understood what he was about and nodded that it was all right.

Turning to Poppy, Calder hugged her fiercely. "I'm sorry," he said softly, but Felicity could hear him.

"I'm so glad you're all right." Poppy pulled back in his embrace and smiled up at him. "You shouldn't be out here."

"I'm the duke. I most definitely should be out here." He kissed her cheek, then turned to Gabriel, offering his hand. "Darlington."

"Probably time you called me Gabriel. If you'd like."

"I would, but only if you'll stop calling me Chill. I never cared for that name."

"Fair enough," Gabriel said.

"I'm glad to see you're feeling better, Your Grace," Mrs. Armstrong said with a curtsey. "They said you were ill."

"I wouldn't miss the St. Stephen's Day party." He flinched. "I suppose I did try, but I've come to my senses now." He smiled at Felicity and took her arm once more. "Thanks to Mrs. Garland, who will soon be Her Grace, the Duchess of Hartwell."

Mrs. Armstrong clapped her hands together. "How wonderful!"

"I wanted to be sure to tell you that I'll be bringing several dogs—and more cats—to Hartwell House. The children need pets."

A small pleat gathered between Mrs. Armstrong's brows. "I have a cat, and there are goats."

"Goats do not make great pets," he said wryly. "You need dogs. And more cats."

"What a marvelous idea!" Poppy said.

"What's that?" Bianca and Ash joined them. She looked to Calder. "You're looking better, brother, but should you really be outside?"

"Felicity is managing me well enough," he said, lifting his free hand in supplication. "Though it sounds as if you and Poppy are helping. I understand you've planned our nuptials."

"It had to be done," Bianca said with a shrug before grinning widely. "That means you said yes?"

"*She* said yes." Calder laughed as he looked from Bianca to Poppy to Felicity. "I fear my life will never be the same." His gaze didn't waver from hers when he softly added, "And for that, I'm eternally grateful."

"What's the idea I missed?" Bianca asked.

Before anyone could answer, Alice, the girl from Hartwell House whom Calder had helped, ran to him and threw her arms around his waist. "They said you were ill."

"I was," he said, taking his arm from Felicity to hug Alice. "But I wouldn't miss the celebration. Are you having fun?" He squatted down to talk to her.

She nodded, her mouth splitting into a wide smile. "I've already beaten Freddie at snapdragon twice." She held up her fingers, which were bright red from pulling raisins from a flaming bowl of brandy.

"Splendid. You'll be delighted to know that Mrs. Armstrong has agreed to let me bring some dogs and cats to Hartwell House next week." He smiled at her. "You shall have the pick of the puppies."

Alice's eyes widened, and she launched herself at him so hard that he lost his balance and fell backward onto the ground. Horrified, Alice leapt up, her jaw dropping. "I'm so sorry, Your Grace!"

Calder lifted his head. "I'm fine."

Felicity rushed to help him, but Ash and Gabriel took charge of restoring him to his feet.

"All right, then?" Ash asked.

Calder clasped his hand in gratitude. "I am, thank you."

"I think you should go back inside," Felicity said, worried that he'd fallen, even if it was only because the girl had jumped at him. "You can sit in the drawing room and watch the festivities from the window."

"I have to make my speech first. The duke always makes a speech."

Felicity was going to argue that his sisters could do it, but Bianca spoke first. "He's right. I'll get everyone's attention."

Calder gave Felicity a look that seemed to imply it was out of his hands, to which Felicity rolled her eyes. She escorted him to the small dais, where Bianca blew a horn.

It took a minute, but conversation died down, and everyone paused in their activities or filed from the tents to look toward the dais.

Calder wiped a hand beneath his eye, but Felicity couldn't see if there had been a tear. She held on to his hand and squeezed him tight, giving him all the strength and love she had.

"Good St. Stephen's Day!" he called out loudly,

surprising Felicity with the volume of his voice considering he'd been ill.

"Welcome to Hartwood. It is my pleasure—our pleasure"—he gestured to the rest of his family on the dais—"to have you here. I would like to start by saying we will have another celebration soon, for I am to wed the lovely woman at my side. May I present the future Duchess of Hartwell." He bowed to Felicity, and she blushed beneath the applause and cheering.

When the congratulations faded, Calder continued. "I want to thank my sisters, Lady Darlington and Lady Buckleigh, for their hard work and dedication to making this celebration happen, and for all they do for Hartwell House and our village."

This was met with more cheering. Poppy and Bianca curtsied on the dais.

After several moments, Calder was able to go on. "I also want to thank Lord Darlington and Lord Buckleigh for their help today and every day. I should also thank Lord Thornaby for his assistance and his willingness to host the party when I was… When I was an idiot."

Gasps and nods spread through the crowd.

"I have no excuse for my behavior since becoming the duke, but I shall promise you here today that the people of Hartwood and Hartwell are my primary concern. I look forward to refurbishing Hartwell House and assisting with the reconstruction of Shield's End. And I want each of you to know that I am here to support you and ensure your welfare."

The cheering and applause started anew and continued apace until Calder held up his hand. "Forgive me, but I need to rest before I collapse—it's true that I am ill. If I don't go inside, I fear my betrothed will drag me." He sent her a loving look. She shook her head at a round of guffaws.

"Before I go," he said, "I want to announce that we will add two new celebrations to the calendar. We will have a May Day Celebration and a Harvest Festival. Now go and enjoy your day!"

The applause and cheers rose to a crescendo, and Calder spent the next half hour shaking people's hands and even giving a few hugs. By the time Felicity wrestled him back inside, she could tell he was quite fatigued.

"Never mind what I said about watching from the drawing room. You're going back to bed."

"Thank God," he said.

"May I help?" Truro asked. The butler had apparently followed them inside. "It appeared as though His Grace could use some assistance."

Calder looked to Truro. "You should be outside celebrating. This is your day," he said.

"I will, but first I want to see you comfortable."

"I don't deserve you, Truro." Calder gazed at him earnestly. "Truly. You've endured a great deal from me these past several months."

"I didn't think it would last, Your Grace. Besides, I put up with your father for far longer, and I'm still here." He winked at Calder. "You'll be fine. And I'm here to help. Come, let's get you upstairs."

Calder allowed them both to help him to his bedchamber, and a short while later, he was resituated in bed. Truro had insisted on having someone brew a pot of tea and promised it would be up shortly.

"Thank you, Truro," Calder called as the butler left. He turned his attention to Felicity. "I really don't deserve him. But I don't deserve you either."

"Please promise me you won't keep saying that."

"Every day for the rest of our lives. I'm afraid you must get used to it."

Isis jumped onto the bed and sat on his feet. She'd accompanied them outside, but had ended up playing with some of the children from Hartwell House. Now, however, she looked quite content to doze on her master's feet and keep him warm.

The tea arrived along with some toast, which Calder hungrily devoured. Then he yawned, and Felicity insisted he should sleep.

"But I've been sleeping for over a day." He yawned again and sank down into the bed, despite his protests.

Felicity tucked him in and kissed his temple.

"Aren't you getting in here with me?" he asked. "You look tired too. I know you can't have slept much."

"That's true." She glanced toward the door. "It's not really proper, though, is it?"

"A betrothal is as good as marriage, and I just announced our betrothal to everyone. Besides, I'm well past following the rules of propriety as far as we're concerned. I'm not spending another moment without you."

After stripping down to her chemise, she climbed into his bed and snuggled up beside him. His breaths were deep and even, and she was fairly certain he was already asleep.

Then he startled her by speaking. His eyes remained closed. "Thank you for rescuing me."

"It wasn't just me."

"Not in the meadow." Now he opened his eyes and turned his head toward her. "From the darkness."

She smiled softly and touched his cheek. "You rescued yourself—you just needed a little help."

"Thankfully I had an angel to help me." He

kissed her forehead, then closed his eyes once more.

Now, she was certain he'd fallen asleep. She murmured, "I think we had angels helping both of us."

EPILOGUE

Christmas Eve 1812

"Is it going to fit?" Bianca asked, cocking her head to the side as Calder hefted the massive Yule log into the hearth with the aid of Gabriel and Ash.

"Maybe?" Felicity said as she stroked her round belly. Calder was practically obsessed with the fact that he was going to be a father. He couldn't stop staring at her.

"Calder, this is very heavy," Gabriel said, drawing his attention back to the matter at hand.

With a grunt, Calder wedged his side into the fireplace. "Set it down."

Gabriel stood on the opposite end and, heaving his side into the fireplace as well, let the log drop onto the coals from last year's log. They'd spread them that morning, taken from the box in which they'd been stored since the day after Epiphany.

The day he and Felicity had wed. What Felicity didn't know was that he'd saved enough coal from that log so they would be able to use a piece for every Christmas. He smiled at the thought, his gaze drifting once more to his beloved.

She stood between Poppy, who held her four-month old son Thaddeus, and Bianca, who was also with child, but not yet obviously so. She and Ash would welcome their babe in the early summer, while his and Felicity's would be here in just a matter of weeks.

He could scarcely believe how drastically his life had changed—and how utterly grateful he was that the future he'd glimpsed was not to be. Or part of it, anyway. If he was the man standing beside Felicity surrounded by their children and grand-children, he would count himself fortunate.

"It fits," Ash said, stepping back to put his arm around Bianca. "Barely."

"That should have no problem lasting through Twelfth Night," Bianca said, pressing against her husband's side.

Calder set to lighting the massive log, which was no small feat. After some time, it began to burn. Everyone cheered, including Felicity's and Ash's mothers, who were also present, and brandy was poured all around.

"To family," Calder said, raising his glass.

Everyone lifted their glasses with a resounding chorus of "Hear, hear!"

Calder assisted Felicity to a settee and sat down beside her. The mothers found chairs, and his sisters gathered on other settees with their husbands.

"My mother says the packing is going well at Hartwell House," Felicity said, glancing toward Alicia Templeton. "I'm sorry I haven't been able to help." She'd been rather tired the past week, and Calder had insisted she not overtax herself. While he wasn't as petrified of pregnancy and childbirth as Gabriel had been, he saw no reason to take unnecessary risks.

"We've had plenty of hands," Poppy said, juggling her son and her brandy glass. "Which is not the case for me right now." She laughed and handed her glass to Gabriel so she could better situate Thaddeus. "We still have a few weeks before Shield's End will be ready to be inhabited."

Indeed, there were many things still to be done, and that was with the hired firm conducting work along with assistance from Calder, Gabriel, Ash, and many other people from Hartwell. It had been a massive community effort, which was the only way the reconstruction could have happened so quickly.

Bianca leaned back against her settee and into her husband. "It can't happen too soon. The school will be taking its first pupils at the beginning of February."

Hartwell House would soon be known as the Hartwell School. They'd intended it to be a day school only, but the interest for boarding had been so great that they'd opened it up to a small number of applicants from County Durham. The spots had filled quickly, and already there was discussion as to how to enlarge the school so they could accept more.

Though young, Dinah Kitson had proved herself an excellent manager for the school. Actually, she hadn't been as young as they'd all assumed. She was, in fact, nearly Poppy's age.

The repairs on Hartwell House had been completed last spring.

"Pardon me for a moment," Poppy said, handing Thaddeus off to his father.

Bianca rose. "Oh yes, me too."

Calder watched in bemusement as they went to

the corner to a small desk. A strong kick from the child in Felicity's womb drew his attention. She looked up at him, her eyes glowing. "He's very active this evening."

"*She* is usually active in the evenings. I fear she will keep us up at night."

"Perhaps." Felicity took his hand and set it on her belly. Another kick landed against his palm.

"Calder, we have something for you," Bianca announced. She and Poppy now stood before him, a box in Poppy's hands.

He blinked at them in confusion. "But we exchanged gifts on St. Nicholas Day. Poppy, you gave me a lovely embroidered waistcoat, and Bianca, you gave me a book."

"Yes, well, this gift wasn't quite finished," Poppy glanced toward her husband, then gave the box to Calder. "It took a long time to find the last piece, and it only just arrived yesterday."

Calder took the box and set it in his lap. He turned his head to look at Felicity. "Do you know anything about this?"

She shook her head. "I do not. But I'm quite interested to see what it is. Do hurry and open it."

The box was a foot long and half as wide. Its height was smaller, perhaps three inches. He would have guessed it was a box for jewelry, but why would they give him such a thing?

The lid was hinged with a small clasp that held it shut. Flipping the clasp open, he lifted the lid. The contents completely stole his breath.

Lying on a bed of brown velvet were his mother's jewels: the emerald necklace, earrings, and ring. He couldn't believe what he was seeing.

He had to blink back the tears blurring his vision as he looked up at his sisters. "Are these real?" he whispered.

They both nodded.

"Ash and Gabriel spent a great deal of time looking for them last Season," Bianca said. "I believe the ring ended up in a rather unsavory place."

Poppy elbowed her, murmuring, "Don't make him feel bad."

"How could I feel bad?" Calder touched the fine jewels, seeing his mother wearing them on Christmas when he was a boy. "This is the greatest gift I've ever received." He looked at Felicity, his heart so full, he feared it would burst. "Except for you and the babe."

She reached over and put her hand over his atop the jewelry. "I know what you meant." She smiled up at her sisters-in-law. "This is truly lovely."

"Well, I can't wear them, obviously," Calder said, angling his body toward Felicity. "And I'd always wanted my wife to have them. When I lost you, I couldn't imagine anyone else wearing them. While I hated to part with the set, I convinced myself that I didn't need it. Not without you."

She lifted her hand and cupped his cheek. "Oh, Calder."

He looked to his sisters. "Do you mind if I give them to Felicity?"

"Of course not," Poppy said, beaming. "We expected you would, and we're delighted for her to have them."

Calder wouldn't have blamed them if they'd wanted to keep the items for themselves. But then they didn't remember their mother, while he did. "Thank you."

He took the necklace from the box and held it up toward Felicity. She pivoted so he could fasten the piece around her neck. When she turned back, tears filled his eyes again.

She wiped her finger across his cheek to catch a teardrop, smiling. "Happy tears, I hope."

"The happiest. Thank you." He turned to his sisters. "Thank you." Then he looked to his brothers-in-law. "Thank you." He wiped at his eyes and glanced toward Felicity's and Ash's mothers, saying, "Thank you too!"

Everyone chuckled. Bianca grinned. "Happy Christmas, Calder."

He put his arm around Felicity and drew her close, pressing a kiss against her temple. "Happy Christmas, everyone."

THE END

THANK YOU!

Thank you so much for reading Joy to the Duke! It's the final book in my Regency holiday series, Love is All Around. I hope you enjoyed the trilogy; I had such fun writing it! If you think some of the secondary characters might need a story and an happy ever after, drop me a note!

Would you like to know when my next book is available and to hear about sales and deals? Sign up for my VIP newsletter at https://www.darcyburke. com/readergroup, follow me on social media: Facebook: https://facebook.com/DarcyBurkeFans
Twitter at @darcyburke
Instagram at darcyburkeauthor
Pinterest at darcyburkewrite

And follow me on Bookbub to receive updates on pre-orders, new releases, and deals!

Need more Regency romance? Check out my other historical series:

The Spitfire Society - Meet the smart, independent women who've decided they don't need Society's rules, their families' expectations, or, most importantly, a husband. But just because they don't need a man doesn't mean they might not *want* one...

The Untouchables - Swoon over twelve of Society's most eligible and elusive bachelor peers and the bluestockings, wallflowers, and outcasts who bring them to their knees!

Wicked Dukes Club - six books written by me and my BFF, NYT Bestselling Author Erica Ridley. Meet the unforgettable men of London's most notorious tavern, The Wicked Duke. Seductively handsome, with charm and wit to spare, one night with these rakes and rogues will never be enough...

Secrets and Scandals - six epic stories set in London's glittering ballrooms and England's lush countryside, and the first one, Her Wicked Ways, is free!

Legendary Rogues - Four intrepid heroines and adventurous heroes embark on exciting quests across Regency England and Wales!

If you like contemporary romance, I hope you'll check out my Ribbon Ridge series available from Avon Impulse, and the continuation of Ribbon Ridge in So Hot.

I hope you'll consider leaving a review at your favorite online vendor or networking site!

I appreciate my readers so much. Thank you, thank you, *thank you.*

AUTHOR NOTE

One day last spring I thought it would be fun to write a Christmas trilogy and base the stories on classic holiday tales. I knew right away I wanted to write The Duke of Scrooge, except Joy to the Duke seemed like a much better title. In fact, I think that title popping into my head was actually the seed that grew into Love is All Around.

The task of writing a rather nasty character who would need to transform into a swoon-worthy hero is actually something I relish. I love, love to read about redemption, and boy is Calder's arc a doozy. In writing a series about siblings, I wanted to explore how their experiences and perspectives can be very different and how we all have our own path to take. Hopefully you enjoyed Calder's and Felicity's.

The Institution for Impoverished Women is something entirely of my own creation. It's based on workhouses of the time, but I didn't want a "real" workhouse which separated men and women (and children—they didn't see their parents often) and was typically more like a prison.

Thanks and love to Rachel Grant for the super

helpful writing sprints and always fabulous friendship.

I hope you enjoyed this inspired story! And Merry Christmas. :)

Wicked Dukes Club

One Night for Seduction by Erica Ridley
One Night of Surrender by Darcy Burke
One Night of Passion by Erica Ridley
One Night of Scandal by Darcy Burke
One Night to Remember by Erica Ridley
One Night of Temptation by Darcy Burke

Secrets and Scandals

Her Wicked Ways
His Wicked Heart
To Seduce a Scoundrel
To Love a Thief (a novella)
Never Love a Scoundrel
Scoundrel Ever After

Legendary Rogues

Lady of Desire
Romancing the Earl
Lord of Fortune
Captivating the Scoundrel

Contemporary Romance

Ribbon Ridge

Where the Heart Is (a prequel novella)
Only in My Dreams
Yours to Hold
When Love Happens
The Idea of You

When We Kiss

You're Still the One

Ribbon Ridge: So Hot

So Good

So Right

So Wrong

The Untouchables Series

THE FORBIDDEN DUKE

"I LOVED this story!!" 5 Stars

-Historical Romance Lover

"This is a wonderful read and I can't wait to see what comes next in this amazing series..." 5 Stars

-Teatime and Books

THE DUKE of DARING

"You will not be able to put it down once you start. Such a good read."

-Books Need TLC

"An unconventional beauty set on life as a spinster meets the one man who might change her mind, only to find his painful past makes it impossible to love. A wonderfully emotional journey from attraction, to friendship, to a love that conquers all."

-Bronwen Evans, *USA Today* Bestselling Author

THE DUKE of DECEPTION

"...an enjoyable, well-paced story ... Ned and Aquilla are an engaging, well-matched couple –

strong, caring and compassionate; and ...it's easy to believe that they will continue to be happy together long after the book is ended."

"This is my favorite so far in the series! They had chemistry from the moment they met...their passion leaps off the pages."

THE DUKE of DESIRE

"Masterfully written with great characterization...with a flourish toward characters, secrets, and romance... Must read addition to "The Untouchables" series!"

"If you are looking for a truly endearing story about two people who take the path least travelled to find the other, with a side of 'YAH THAT'S HOT!' then this book is absolutely for you!"

THE DUKE of DEFIANCE

"This story was so beautifully written, and it hooked me from page one. I couldn't put the book down and just had to read it in one sitting even though it meant reading into the wee hours of the morning."

"I loved the Duke of Defiance! This is the kind of book you hate when it is over and I had to make myself stop reading just so I wouldn't have to leave the fun of Knighton's (aka Bran) and Joanna's story!"

-Behind Closed Doors Book Review

THE DUKE of DANGER

"The sparks fly between them right from the start... the HEA is certainly very hard-won, and well-deserved."

-All About Romance

"Another book hangover by Darcy! Every time I pick a favorite in this series, she tops it. The ending was perfect and made me want more."

-Sassy Book Lover

THE DUKE of ICE

"Each book gets better and better, and this novel was no exception. I think this one may be my fave yet! 5 out 5 for this reader!"

-Front Porch Romance

"An incredibly emotional story...I dare anyone to stop reading once the second half gets under way because this is intense!"

-Buried Under Romance

THE DUKE of RUIN

"This is a fast paced novel that held me until the last page."

" ...everything I could ask for in a historical romance... impossible to stop reading."

THE DUKE of LIES

"THE DUKE OF LIES is a work of genius! The characters are wonderfully complex, engaging; there is much mystery, and so many, many lies from so many people; I couldn't wait to see it all uncovered."

"..the epitome of romantic [with]...a bit of danger/action. The main characters are mature, fierce, passionate, and full of surprises. If you are a hopeless romantic and you love reading stories that'll leave you feeling like you're walking on clouds then you need to read this book or maybe even this entire series."

THE DUKE of SEDUCTION

"There were tears in my eyes for much of the last 10% of this book. So good!"

"An absolute joy to read... I always recommend Darcy!"

-Brittany and Elizabeth's Book Boutique

THE DUKE of KISSES

"Don't miss this magnificent read. It has some comedic fun, heartfelt relationships, heartbreaking moments, and horrifying danger."

-The Reading Café

"...my favorite story in the series. Fans of Regency romances will definitely enjoy this book."

-Two Ends of the Pen

THE DUKE of DISTRACTION

"Count on Burke to break a heart as only she can. This couple will get under the skin before they steal your heart."

-Hopeless Romantic

"Darcy Burke never disappoints. Her storytelling is just so magical and filled with passion. You will fall in love with the characters and the world she creates!"

-Teatime and Books

Secrets & Scandals Series

HER WICKED WAYS

"A bad girl heroine steals both the show and a highwayman's heart in Darcy Burke's deliciously wicked debut."

–Courtney Milan, *NYT* Bestselling Author

"…fast paced, very sexy, with engaging characters."

–*Smexybooks*

HIS WICKED HEART

"Intense and intriguing. Cinderella meets *Fight Club* in a historical romance packed with passion, action and secrets."

–Anna Campbell, *Seven Nights in a Rogue's Bed*

"A romance...to make you smile and sigh…a wonderful read!"

–*Rogues Under the Covers*

TO SEDUCE A SCOUNDREL

"Darcy Burke pulls no punches with this sexy, romantic page-turner. Sevrin and Philippa's story grabs you from the first scene and doesn't let go. *To Seduce a Scoundrel* is simply delicious!"

–Tessa Dare, *NYT* Bestselling Author

"I was captivated on the first page and didn't let go until this glorious book was finished!"

–*Romancing the Book*

TO LOVE A THIEF

"With refreshing circumstances surrounding both the hero and the heroine, a nice little mystery, and a touch of heat, this novella was a perfect way to pass the day."

–The Romanceaholic

"A refreshing read with a dash of danger and a little heat. For fans of honorable heroes and fun heroines who know what they want and take it."

-The Luv NV

NEVER LOVE A SCOUNDREL

"I loved the story of these two misfits thumbing their noses at society and finding love." Five stars.

–A Lust for Reading

"A nice mix of intrigue and passion...wonderfully complex characters, with flaws and quirks that will draw you in and steal your heart."

–BookTrib

SCOUNDREL EVER AFTER

"There is something so delicious about a bad boy, no matter what era he is from, and Ethan was definitely delicious."

-A Lust for Reading

"I loved the chemistry between the two main characters...Jagger/Ethan is not what he seems at all and neither is sweet society Miss Audrey. They are believably compatible."

-Confessions of a College Angel

Legendary Rogues Series

LADY of DESIRE

"A fast-paced mixture of adventure and romance, very much in the mould of *Romancing the Stone* or *Indiana Jones*."

-*All About Romance*

"...gave me such a book hangover! ...addictive...one of the most entertaining stories I've read this year!"

-*Adria's Romance Reviews*

ROMANCING the EARL

"Once again Darcy Burke takes an interesting story and...turns it into magic. An exceptionally well-written book."

-*Bodice Rippers, Femme Fatale, and Fantasy*

"...A fast paced story that was exciting and interesting. This is a definite must add to your book lists!"

-*Kilts and Swords*

LORD of FORTUNE

"I don't think I know enough superlatives to describe this book! It is wonderfully, magically delicious. It sucked me in from the very first sentence and didn't turn me loose—not even at the end ..."

-*Flippin Pages*

"If you love a deep, passionate romance with a bit of mystery, then this is the book for you!"
  -Teatime and Books

CAPTIVATING the SCOUNDREL

"I am in absolute awe of this story. Gideon and Daphne stole all of my heart and then some. This book was such a delight to read."

-*Beneath the Covers Blog*

"Darcy knows how to end a series with a bang! Daphne and Gideon are a mix of enemies and allies turned lovers that will have you on the edge of your seat at every turn."

-*Sassy Booklover*

Contemporary Romance

Ribbon Ridge Series

A contemporary family saga featuring the Archer family of sextuplets who return to their small Oregon wine country town to confront tragedy and find love...

The "multilayered plot keeps readers invested in the story line, and the explicit sensuality adds to the excitement that will have readers craving the next Ribbon Ridge offering."

"Darcy Burke writes a uniquely touching and heart-warming series about the love, pain, and joys of family as well as the love that feeds your soul when you meet "the one.""

I can't tell you how much I love this series. Each book gets better and better.

"Darcy Burke's Ribbon Ridge series is one of my all-time favorites. Fall in love with the Archer family, I know I did."

Ribbon Ridge: So Hot

SO GOOD

" ...worth the read with its well-written words, beautiful descriptions, and likeable characters...they are flirty, sexy and a match made in wine heaven."

"I absolutely love the characters in this book and

the families. I honestly could not put it down and finished it in a day."

SO RIGHT

"This is another great story by Darcy Burke. Painting pictures with her words that make you want to sit and stare at them for hours. I love the banter between the characters and the general sense of fun and friendliness."

" ...the romance is emotional; the characters are spirited and passionate... "

SO WRONG

"As usual, Ms. Burke brings you fun characters and witty banter in this sweet hometown series. I loved the dance between Crystal and Jamie as they fought their attraction."

"I really love both this series and the Ribbon Ridge series from Darcy Burke. She has this way of taking your heart and ripping it right out of your chest one second and then the next you are laughing at something the characters are doing."

ABOUT THE AUTHOR

Darcy Burke is the USA Today Bestselling Author of sexy, emotional historical and contemporary romance. Darcy wrote her first book at age 11, a happily ever after about a swan addicted to magic and the female swan who loved him, with exceedingly poor illustrations. Join her Reader Club at https://www.darcyburke.com/readerclub.

A native Oregonian, Darcy lives on the edge of wine country with her guitar-strumming husband, their two hilarious kids who seem to have inherited the writing gene. They're a crazy cat family with two Bengal cats, a small, fame-seeking cat named after a fruit, and an older rescue Maine Coon who is the master of chill and five a.m. serenading. In her "spare" time Darcy is a serial volunteer enrolled in a 12-step program where one learns to say "no," but she keeps having to start over. Her happy places are Disneyland and Labor Day weekend at the Gorge. Visit Darcy online at https://www.darcyburke.com and follow her social media: Facebook at http://www.facebook.com/darcyburkefans, Twitter @darcyburke at https://www.twitter.com/darcyburke, Instagram at https://www.instagram/darcyburkeauthor, and Pinterest at https://www.pinterest.com/darcyburkewrite.

CPSIA information can be obtained
at www.ICGtesting.com
Printed in the USA
BVHW071724240220
573160BV00010B/1435

9 781944 576677